Second Time Around

and other stories

The Timely Birth of a Somewhat Comic Character

Second Time Around and Other Stories comprises five stories in which the semi-comic hero, Ludwig Fried, looks for romance and meaning (personal and historical) in his home base, Western New York, Kansas, Dubai (en route), and Myanmar. Ludwig is a restless loner, dreamer, humanitarian, introspective writer, and 20th century embodiment of Jewish history who longs for security and thinks he needs to travel to find it. Ludwig lives in the shadow of many histories, including that of a street-smart father, a latent dreamer. Ludwig's mission is to move out of the shadows of the Holocaust, paternal anxiety, academic orthodoxies, literary hierarchies, and romantic uncertainties (leavened with eros) into the light of a self-acceptance that allows him to reach out fully to others and to welcome them with open arms. Ludwig's moods and ruminations waver between stand-up comedy one-liners and the interiority of Henry James. If it were possible, Ludwig would like to arrive at a philosophy of life that combined the lyrics of Frank Sinatra's songs and the wisdom of Montaigne. Howard R. Wolf, the author, has learned more from Ludwig than Ludwig has learned from his creator. This may tell us something about one function of literature: we learn to live better and more interesting lives by imagining worlds in which to live. Every story ends with the possibility for a new beginning. Like the bagel, life is a circle.

AUTHOR

Howard R. Wolf is Emeritus Professor and Senior Fellow in the Department of English at SUNY-Buffalo. A graduate of Horace Mann School, Amherst College (B.A.), Columbia University (M.A.), and The University of Michigan (Ph.D.) where he was a Hopwood winner, he has been a Fulbright scholar in Turkey (1983-84) and South Africa (1998). He is Life-Member of Wolfson College, Cambridge University and PEN America. His academic fields are American Literature, Autobiography, Short Fiction, Literary Journalism and the Essay. His published creative work has been in the areas of memoir and the personal essay, short fiction, novel, literary and social criticism, letters, humor, travel, education, and drama. His book publications are: *Upper Manhattan: A Family Album* (poems, 1990); *Forgive the Father: A Memoir of Changing Generations* (1978); *The Education of a Teacher* (essays, 1987); *A Version of Home: Letters from the World*; *Broadway Serenade* (novel, 1996); *The Education of Ludwig Fried* (Jewish American stories, 2006), *Far-Away Places: Lessons in Exile* (travel essays, 2007). His essays have appeared in: *Midstream, The Nation; Christian Science Monitor*, *The New Republic; The American Scholar; The Virginia Quarterly, The Sewanee Review,* and *Cithara: Essays in The Judeo-Christian Tradition.* His short stories have appeared in *Commonwealth Review, Evening Street Review, Nimrod, Mediterranean Review, Cimmaron Review,* and *Pleiades*. Three related one-acts--"Reunion of a Summer Evening," "Blue Nights in South Florida," and "Unveiling at Twilight in the Hotel De Dream"—were published under the title *Home at the End of the Day,* by Prestige Books International (Delhi, India) in 2017. Special Collections in the Frost Library (Amherst College) holds an archive of his literary career and the work of his contemporaries. Professor Wolf has presented over 100 lectures all together in twenty countries.

Second Time Around

and other stories

The Timely Birth of a Somewhat Comic Character

Howard R. Wolf

Prestige Books International
New Delhi

Published by
Prestige Books International
New Delhi 110 060
prestigebooks@gmail.com
Phone: 9818755529

Associate Office
11B, Broomwood Road
London SW11 6HU

Associate Office
P.O. Box 2250
Sydney 2001

ISBN: 978-81-938503-8-1

Printed in India

Contents

Preface

I had been working on a series of stories about one Jewish American character, "Ludwig Fried," since 2004 when I learned that a great uncle by the same name had been killed in a Nazi concentration camp in 1942. This tragic news changed my life and life as a writer. I no longer could regard my life-struggles and disappointments with as much seriousness as I had up to that point. If I were going to use my experience as the basis for creating a protagonist, a version of my identity, that character would have to be dramatized in somewhat comic terms. "He" would have to be a persona whose picaresque journey through life, however problematic and beset with challenges, would have to be both diminished and enlarged by an implicit comparison with the tragedy of the Holocaust. I meant to write one story about *him*, "Library of the Lost," but that story opened a door into his imagined psyche that opened other doors. Each story seemed to bring him to the end of a quest for self-knowledge that required a new beginning, another path up a mountain that might reach a lookout where he could stand and say, "I have extracted as much meaning from *my* history as possible and must leave it to readers to decide if it has sufficient weight *after* our knowledge of the death-camps, Hiroshima, and genocides." Readers interested in a longer treatment of the story behind my cycle of "Ludwig" stories are encouraged to read the "Afterword."

Three of these stories have been published earlier. "The Icicles of Eggertsville" was first published in the January 2017 issue of *The Commonwealth Review* (India). "At the Edge of the West" was first published in the Spring 2018 issue of *Trajectory* (Kentucky). "Second Time Around" was first published in the Spring 2019 issue of *Evening Street Review* (California).

HOWARD R. WOLF
Blue Spruce House, Amherst, N.Y.

At the Edge of the West

Ludwig Fried—small-time college teacher, wannabe big-time writer, occasional victim, addict of the unattainable, a wondering and wandering American Jew—was tired of being Ludwig Fried, but who else could he be or become at his age and stage of life? At any age or stage, for that matter? Did he or anyone else really have an option, even in an age of options, when it came to identity, a word that had been inscribed on the psyche of his generation, the 1950s, like an invisible tattoo? More invisible than dye, but there it was, an ineradicable, if unseen, marker: The Scarlett "I" emblazoned on his soul.

If thinking about the house of his selfhood (its Poe-like dank tarn, no sump-pump available) could wear out a person, it was one reason why Ludwig now felt exhausted as he lay in late April at the edge of a wheat field in Liberty, Kansas, itself an emptied town, his New York snoot, like Durante's, pressed into the loam. Only a ripple of wind from the west, stirring the remaining Rembrandt-golden stalks, kept him awake and positioned, perhaps, to imagine a new life.

Yes, it had been a long and exhausting trip for him: flying from Buffalo through O'Hare to Tulsa, renting a car with a malfunctioning GPS, and driving up through the oil fields and Bible Belt signs of Oklahoma to the tiny, once oil rich town of Liberty in southeast Kansas; but it wasn't the drive itself that made him want to lie down for a semi-snooze on the stubble-harvested field. *It's me*, he thought.

He had been picking at his inner life for so long that he felt like one of the praying mantis-like derricks he had seen on either side of Route 75 driving up from Tulsa. They lifted and lowered their arms every few seconds as he had pecked at a typewriter for years, a literary woodpecker.

He had been trying to hit pay dirt by drilling into himself, hoping for a gusher of insight, but his bit had lost its edge. He needed to get another tool or give up drilling. He needed to find a way out of self-examination, and maybe *Out* was the way: the open road, Jack Kerouac, the Prairie, Go West, not so young scribbler: not *In*, inner light, Freud on Park Avenue. Scratching and pecking for black gold in the wildcat fields of self-consciousness just hadn't struck a gusher for Ludwig.

After all, he hadn't left the East to come to the prairie, the edge of the West, just to attend an academic hoedown in order to present a paper on the plays of William Inge at a theater festival in a Kansas town, Liberty, the writer's birthplace, so small that Arby's was considered a gourmet restaurant. The paper, like a literary firefly, would emit light for a second and then go dark.

It was too bad that Inge, poor guy, a suicide, whose short-lived fame failed to be a remedy for loneliness, hadn't lived long enough to witness something like a revival. Maybe that would have saved him. *After all, I only need an arrival*, Ludwig thought.

Not that he didn't think well of Kansas. His greatest college buddy, one of Thomas Jefferson's natural aristocrats, had come from Hutchinson. In fact, half the reason for coming to Kansas had been to pay homage to his college roommate of yore, Miller "Spike" Wesley, now CEO of Hallmark Cards in Kansas City. Spike had opened up the West for him, if only in imagination until now. For years, he had daydreamed, especially during the *longeur* of department meetings, about Western Meadowlarks, sunflowers, and cottonwood, to say nothing of wooden windmills creaking in the wind. Not that many wooden windmills were left—like the dial telephone, Jamesian paragraphs, and his hairline, they were vanishing.

No, he was looking for a new life, or a new edition of his old life, or a blending of the two, or the simultaneous existence of two lives. He wanted to pour the old wine of Ludwig Fried into a new bottle: to transform himself from a semi-loser at love into a part-time Romeo, from a minor writer with major anxieties into a major writer with minor anxieties.

He was tired of one-month stands and daily rejections by major publishers. He wanted and needed to be accepted in the two ways that could fulfill a writer if he was a man, and *yes*, he had to admit it, despite extreme Feminism—he *was* a man, gender-wise. He couldn't fit the LBGTQ scheme of things, but *I still have needs*, he thought.

The child of an ill-fated marriage between a hustling garment manufacturer and a naïve girl from the slagheaps of a railroad town near Altoona, PA, Ludwig had been wary of intimacy from the get-go. But he had tried marriage once and failed, and then, after many years of loneliness, had been saved, so he thought, by a sporty young spirit from Buffalo with Pre-Raphaelite tresses, whom he amused, he thought, and who would be his *amuse-gueule* and muse. Instead, she emptied his tank and left him stranded on the I-90 between Ithaca and Buffalo. Not the "trail of tears," but related to it.

Blue balls in adolescence had been painful enough, but the black and blue balls of the heart were even worse. He had begun to wear an emotional codpiece as a defense. He knew this about himself, but he had, in short, and in BVDs, become anxious about closeness. A son of the Garment Center, he had traded his father's bolts of blue gabardine for literary and romantic bolts from the blue, and he had been hit by a bolt of lightning at the deepest vanishing point of his ego.

Ludwig needed to move on, to find new ways to write and love. That's why, looking for a fresh start, he had come to Kansas. It was ironic that he had come to Liberty as he was on the verge of giving up inner-drilling since the town itself once had been the epicenter of an oil and gas boom in the first decade of the 20th century, a boom reflected in Inge's screenplay for *Splendor in the Grass*. Ludwig would settle for *Splenda*, a "lite" romance, some stirring of the heart and loins.

It might be possible to lead two lives or two versions of the same life without cracking up. Freud had given ambivalence a bad name, but maybe the equation could be reversed. If fusion wasn't possible for Ludwig, *fission might be*, he thought as he pushed his woodpecker beak deeper into the loam beneath the stubble, to become, somehow, a man both of the East and West, an obverse and reverse Self, a doppelganger unto himself.

Perhaps it was simpler: Ludwig just needed a new woman in his life, someone he might meet in Kansas, to look at differently, or just to look at him. It had been some time since he had been the object of some youngish woman's adoring gaze. Unlike most of the contemporary French croissant-type critics, he didn't mind being the object of a stare, especially if he could be the glint in the eye of a daughter of the Plains.

It was risky to set out in quest of a new life, but, again, who knew what history had in store for you if you stayed in one place and didn't flee when threats appeared on the horizon? Look what had happened in Germany on *Kristallnacht* when the Brown Shirts smashed the windows of merchants and the shopkeepers thought, "Well, I can find another location." A new location had been found for them, and it usually was . . . the last one.

What was Ludwig risking, in any case, by looking for a new version of himself in Kansas? He wasn't burning any bridges that couldn't be rebuilt in a few visits to Home Depot. He was an itinerant Lecturer of English, an archaic title, still untenured, at a small college in the orbit of Buffalo, a lesser digit of the Finger Lakes.

But here he was ruminating and idling instead of letting the rich scent of the threshed field fill his Bronx nostrils with sensuous expectation and the kind of optimism that had made "Oklahoma" such a hit in the New York of his youth.

The words of the musical never had been out of his cranial concert hall for too long. "There's a bright golden haze on the meadow, there's a bright golden haze on the meadow, the corn is as high as an el-e-phant's eye, an' it looks like . . . Oh, what a beautiful morn . . ."

Now he was in the real West, his Bronx nose pressed into moist loam and stubble.

Though still lingering, he had checked in at the Moonglow Motel at one end of the field where he lay. It was the place to stay along with the other conferees, mainly actors from LA, Chicago, and New York. An illuminated fountain in the shape of a sunflower bubbled in the lobby. It was, he hoped, an augury of life rolling with new energy.

It soon would be time for the welcoming ceremony in Liberty's community library. The conference coincided with a local festival, known as "Neewollah," Halloween spelled backwards, a mirror of his life. He heard the sound of a band, probably a high school marching unit, coming from the college's end of the field. He assumed they were tuning up for the opening of the theater festival, an annual event that enlivened the townspeople of Liberty.

Now he had to go to the motel and get dressed, and here he was still stuck in a middle zone, the fifty-yard line of ambivalence. No Prufrock, he wasn't paralyzed. He could act, depending how you defined it. Ludwig stood, pulled a few stalks of wheat from his ears, and ambled towards the Moonglow Motel. Somehow, his gait felt freer, younger. *Maybe Western*, he thought.

As he walked across the field towards the gussied up motel, "inn" to the theater crowd, he saw a gathering of dark clouds in the west and—he wasn't sure—the faint outline of a spiral. There had been tornado warnings, so he quickened his pace, not easy for a man with chronic sciatica. Then, as he got to the edge of the field, the clouds parted and bright pitchfork-sharp rays lit up the face of a young woman, late thirties, who also had been taking the measure of the ominous-looking clouds.

She wore a long gingham dress and seemed to have a garland of lavender placed neatly on top of her plaited hair. It was clear to him: she was no product of the Actor's Studio. She belonged to the land if ever anyone did, and he wondered if he could belong to her.

Suddenly, he was standing next to her.

"Tornado?" he asked.

"Don't think so, there's no yellowish tint in the sky."

"Like a Van Gogh," he said, trying to make an impression.

"Not that vivid," she said.

He was impressed.

"Have you seen the originals?"

"Once, long ago, on a senior high school trip from Fort Scott to Amsterdam, long ago and far-away."

"You're too young for it to have been long ago."

"You'd be surprised. I've been teaching high school drama for fifteen years and have a ten-year-old daughter. Miranda wants to go to New York when she grows up and become an actress. She's already starred in *Annie*."

"Where do you teach?"

"Fort Scott High School, never left after my own days there, went to the Community College, inherited the family farm, two thousand acres. My husband works it, a good man. And you? An actor, I suppose?"

"No, I teach playwriting and, Yahweh, save me, Theory of the Navel, I mean Novel," he chuckled. "At a small college in the Finger Lakes, Keuka. Ever heard of it?"

"Only Cayuga, always wanted to see it. Maybe one day, if there's a good harvest. We need to buy our own combine. Timing is everything when the wheat is ready for harvest. If we wait for a crew following the wheat from Oklahoma to Nebraska, we may lose a chance for a bumper crop."

"I know what you mean. I've got a lawn mower. Never works after a rain."

She laughed.

"We better hurry," she said. "We'll miss the opening ceremony. Sidney Haynick is going to talk about his *Scribbler on the Roof* at some point, I think. Can't miss that, we're doing it this year. Maybe I'll see you later?"

"I'll look for you. Oh, what's your name? Can't tell the actors without a Playbill."

She smiled. "Lizzie, Lizzie Walton."

"Sounds like *Little House on the Prairie*?"

"Wrong series, but almost . . . and it's not too far from here."

"Your house?"

"The 'little house.'"

"I'd like to see it," he said.

"I have a jalopy, maybe there'll be a break tomorrow, and we'll have a chance to see it . . . maybe. We better get gussied up."

"*Jalopy*," the Western word made his heart race.

She adjusted her garland and headed for the motel. He lingered, checked the horizon line in the west—still clear and bright with some gathering clouds in the distance—and followed her.

The sunlight fell on her as she walked away. For a second, Ludwig Fried thought she was a Renoir painting come to life. At least a Norman Rockwell as backup. Any uplifting image might come to mind for this son of the Bronx who had grown up in small and shadowy apartments in early childhood until his father closed a big deal with J.C. Penny. They then moved to Upper Manhattan, Washington Heights, with a view of the Hudson River as wide as this Kansas landscape. The George Washington Bridge had been a sign: Gateway to the West.

Back in his room, Ludwig napped for a while, dreaming of a major review of his latest book in *The New York Times Book Review:* "Ludwig Fried's *Exiles by Starlight and Other Illuminating Displacements* redefines, to some extent, the role of marginal man in Western New York, a partial triumph of the provincial imagination . . . gives cosmopolitan consciousness a run for the money, if not the jackpot . . ."

A semi-anxiety dream, it woke him up and he realized that he was running late, but not running. Half an hour later, he found one of the few empty chairs in the rear of Liberty's Main Library, one of the many libraries that Carnegie had endowed in his bid for name recognition. The room was crowded. Many of the town's civic leaders, teachers, Kiwanis Club members, and donors had joined the conferees for the welcoming remarks by the mayor of Liberty to be followed by an opening talk ("Repression, Suppression, and Freedom in late plays of William Inge: Psychoanalysis as a Democratic Tool").

It was to be presented by Professor Holland Murray, formerly of Columbia University and Director of the Otto Rank Birth Trauma Institute (Greenwich Village Branch). It was to be followed by some comments by Sidney Haynick, famous lyricist of *Scribbler on the Roof.* A banquet would follow.

The title almost made sense to Ludwig. He once had been deep into depth psychology, a cave dweller of the unconscious, but he wanted to tell Lizzie that the dense fog of literary criticism was behind him, that he was surfacing for a breath of fresh Kansas air. He wondered how the townspeople and Lizzie would respond to Murray's talk. After all, they had worked with real tools—spades, trowels, pitchforks. He looked around the room to see if he could spot her. If she was wearing her garland still, though unlikely, it would be easy. He scanned the room and then he saw her sitting between two bald men.

A straw hat with a blue ribbon, resting on her back, highlighted her hair. It was like a meadow, and it gave off something like a "bright golden haze." She was hoping, he thought, to be cast in a Broadway musical. He had to bite his lips to prevent himself from breaking into song. Sitting between two bald men, whose broad Midwestern pates reflected the fading sunlight, added an aura to Lizzie's already spectral appearance to him at this moment—a 4-H angel.

The Mayor's remarks were brief and cordial as he welcomed "thespians and other theater folks to honor William Inge, son of Kansas and the Great Plains, who had put Liberty on the map as the Puritans had made Plymouth Rock a site of national pilgrimage . . ."

Over the top, Ludwig thought, but not wholly untrue. After all, here they were, quite a gathering of New York and LA glitterati in the middle of the prairie that was somewhere at least one week a year. But maybe it was better to be in a new nowhere than where he had been, an old nowhere. Wasn't that the story of America, a new man in an unsettled world?

Professor Murray stepped up to the podium. Seersucker suit neatly pressed, Brooks Bros. pima cotton shirt open at the collar in the spirit of the Plains, he looked around the room slowly as if to say, "I want to make sure everyone is paying attention."

His gaze seemed to pause when he came to Lizzie as if she were the epicenter of the provincial consciousness whose core he wanted to penetrate. Lizzie moved nervously as his eyes rested on her.

"Citizens of Liberty," he began, as if he were about to deliver the *Serment du Jeu de Paume* to the 576 members of the Third estate in Versailles who had been locked out of the Estates-General on June 20, 1789.

Dr. Murray paused, sensing tension and expectation in the hall, no less so than it had been on the eve of the French Revolution when the Tennis Court Oath was pledged to usher in a new era of The Rights of Man. So far as Professor Murray was concerned, the air was as electrically charged as it had been in the last days of Louis XVI. And it occurred to Ludwig with some apprehension that the air over the surrounding wheat fields was, in fact, electrically charged in advance of what might be a severe storm, even a tornado.

"Good citizens of Liberty, colleagues, and devotees of the Great White Way, it's never easy for me to leave my couch, so to speak," he said, smiling. "Not that I'm a potato" (he inserted, smiling more broadly), "but I am flattered and honored to be able to be here today to tell you, as Dr. Freud said, 'Where there was Id, let there be Ego.'"

"Sigmund was right," he continued, as if the Jacques Cousteau of the unconscious had been his snorkeling buddy, "but we must not forget the power of the Id. It must be satisfied somehow. Otherwise, we will have to pay a price—hallucinations, witch hunts, mass delusions. I needn't remind you of *Kristallnacht*, those terrible nights of November 9 and 10, 1938, when Austria and Germany turned against good Jewish citizens, many of whom had sung drinking songs at Heidelberg, dueled, and served in the Kaiser's army during World War One."

As "Holly" scanned the hall, he sensed lack of comprehension or perhaps too much. He needed to lighten up, he thought, to reach them, "I hope I am not being too glib or frivolous when I say that *The lid must be taken off the Id.*"

He smiled smugly, pleased with his turn of phrase, even though he saw no smile or heard no laughter, paused again, and panned the audience as if his eyes were a 35 mm Kinoton movie projector to see if his words had stirred the audience. The audience seemed quieter, a little tense, eager, but anxious to know what he would say next about what they assumed, in a manner of speaking, was Freud's psychological basement. After all, they shopped at Wal-Mart.

Ludwig looked to see how Lizzie might be reacting, but twilight had deepened and ominous clouds, like gray elephants, were all he could see through the arched windows, except for a thin zigzag tracery of lightning in the west. He couldn't see the outlines of Lizzie's blue ribbon.

He wasn't sure which might come first, a tornado that would make them all scurry to the basement of the library or a penetration of the unconscious so deep that it would cause the good citizens of Liberty to flee and seek psychological shelter amid the healthy scents of the cow stalls in the nearby sheds, if not to seek treatment at the Menninger Clinic in Topeka.

As if to activate a sector of the brain that would be capable of answering a question about the brain itself, Professor Murray pressed his digit finger against his temple, then virtually thundered, even as he cracked half a smile, "We now must ask what and *where* is the Id? Yes, the *where* is important, location is everything!"

At the word "where," Ludwig could see heads turning this way and that, up and down. The crowd seemed to be looking for the Id.

"I ask again, *where*?"

Heads continued to swivel around.

"I cannot emphasize this enough," he exclaimed, "and it might not be inappropriate in this time and of this place, to ask in German, for after all, the only prize Dr. Freud ever had conferred on him in his native land was the Goethe Prize—*wohin*?"

But just at that instant, when it seemed that he might be losing the crowd, a spectacular arc of lightning lit up the sky. It was instantaneously followed by an ear-deadening thunderclap that sounded as if it were saying—"*Hier! Hier!*"

How ironic that nature's answer to Murray's question should come from above, not below, the unfinished basement of the mind, but it was a powerful force.

Professor Murray looked pleased.

"At least someone was listening," he said, smiling. "But let me continue my descent into the underworld of the mind as it manifests itself in what I understand to be your festival of *Neewollah*, a going 'down' into the 'up' that Dante and your very own William Inge understood and rendered so poignantly in his *Splendor in the Grass*. "

Murray paused again. Another bolt of lightning lit up the hall and seemed to be aimed at Lizzie. A clap of thunder, followed by a strong wind, sent a few straw hats into the air, swept across the auditorium from west to east, and then reversed itself east to west, as if the hall itself was the Great Plains.

Then there was calm. Ludwig hoped Dr. Murray would wrap up his high-class mumbo-jumbo and let Sidney Haynick speak. A veteran Vegas stand-up and lyricist of Off-Broadway musicals, Haynick could be counted on to put the audience in a good mood for dinner. If Ludwig was lucky, he might be able to sit next to Lizzie and continue something like a micro-flirtation, despite all the polarities and telephone poles between Keuka and Liberty that would make it virtually impossible for them to come together.

Dr. Murray then stretched out his arms as if to say, "It's all right, folks, the storm has passed, just a few more minutes of my *sturm und drang* and I'll turn the podium over to our ever-popular Sidney Haynick." It did look as if calm had been restored, but just then Lizzie—he was sure it was her—stood into a half crouch, passed through her aisle, and rushed past Ludwig who, sitting at the end of his row, was able, unobtrusively, slouching like Groucho, to follow her out the door of the library onto the top of the marble steps.

He snagged the ribbon of her bonnet and held it lightly.

"What's the matter? You'll miss the best part, Haynick will be amusing."

"I've got to go. It's your world, not mine. It's too deep. I don't know much about the 'Id,' and I don't speak German."

Ludwig looked at her sympathetically. "He's just being a pretentious Easterner. Don't worry, he may not even understand what he's saying."

"I don't belong here, Ludwig. Go back in. You came a long way. You don't want to miss anything."

"Okay, I will, but I need to talk to you later. I've got an idea."

She paused. "I'm confused. And tempted to drive back to the farm tonight, but, okay, I'll wait. I'll meet you after the banquet at the edge of the field where we met. I've got some play scripts to read for class, *Our Town* and *Desire under the Elms*."

"Your confusion matches mine," he said. "Midnight it is, edge of the field. Promise?"

She hesitated and then cupped both of his hands in hers as if she were closing the deal on the sale of a thresher. "It's not wise, but I'll be at the edge of the field unless there's lightning and then you'll find me on the verandah facing the field."

She let go of him a little reluctantly, it seemed, and walked down the steps. Ludwig was tempted to follow, but sensed it might be over-zealous, too needy, and re-entered the hall.

Murray had just concluded, "Ich bin ein Kansan this *nacht* . . ."

Ludwig rushed out. As he approached the Moonglow Motel, he felt somewhat hopeful that Lizzie would be waiting for him, as late as it was. So much separated them, but there also appeared to be an attraction, like a magnet. His personality filings were Eastern, hers Western, but each wanted some of the other's filament. Wasn't this also the story of America?

Some kind of escape from the old self and a leap into a new inner harvest might be possible with Lizzie . . . here . . . at the edge of the West. Of course, everything was on spec, they hadn't even embraced; but he felt that their mirror neurons had been reflecting each other . . . and when wasn't romance like two strangers in the night *exchanging glances*?

He checked the horizon line. There were flashes of lightning to the north, more like the pulses of a firefly than bolts. The storm seemed to be moving away, but it still could be dangerous. He assumed Lizzie would be waiting for him under the verandah that faced the open field, not at the edge of the field itself.

As he approached, he saw Lizzie's profile, a silhouette against the glow of a hurricane lantern. She looked like a daguerreotype, and he wondered for a second if the figure he saw was a projection of his inner camera obscura. But as he got closer, he saw that it *was* Lizzie. It surprised him that she was smoking. It didn't fit his image of her.

"You look like Bette Davis," he said.

"I feel like her, I'm nervous, but it's not a movie."

"The storm? It seems to be passing, but what do I know about tornados?"

"My nerves—what did he call it, *sturm und drang*?" she said, putting out the cigarette.

"I don't get it."

"The storm in my Kansas soul and breast. Look how it's heaving."

"It's hard to see, let me borrow a match."

She smiled. "Here, you can help calm me down." She leaned against Ludwig and put her arms around him as if he were a telephone pole. "Can you feel my heart beating? It feels like a pneumatic drill."

He lightly rested his ear on her breast and listened to her heart. "What's the matter, Lizzie? Why are you so upset?"

"I don't belong here, Ludwig. You do, but it's not my world. I couldn't understand Professor Murray, all that fuss about the unconscious, those German words. I'm just a farm girl with a teaching certificate. My life is settled. I don't want to get plowed up."

"Relax. Look, he wasn't making much sense, you're not *just* a farm girl, and I'm tired of that old Viennese talk. Been there, done that. I want to spend some time with you. I'll lean towards you, you'll lean towards me, and we'll meet in the middle, a two person Transcontinental Railroad. We'll drive in the Golden Spike together."

She seemed a little calmer and reminded him of Kim Novak in *Picnic*. He hoped he was becoming her William Holden moving to the rhythms of "Moonglow."

"See how much you know?" she said. "Be realistic. You're trying to make me into a French mistress, but we're both settled, we're both trapped."

"I have an idea, Liz, something may be possible."

"What could be possible other than chaos?"

"See? You know about the uncertainty principle. You're not just a farm girl and look! The storm has passed. Maybe it's an omen."

She stepped out from under the verandah and scanned the sky. The last wispy clouds parted like a Victoria's Secret bra and revealed the moon. "You're right," she said, "it's now as bright as it ever gets. The storm clears out all the humidity. I'll bet we could count all the haystacks in the field."

"Why don't we? Let's take a walk."

"Why not? This will probably be our last time together."

"Aren't you staying tomorrow? Things are just getting started."

"I don't know. I'm not sure. I don't belong here, but let's take that walk and sit on the highest haystack. We can get above everything . . . at least for a moment."

This lifted his spirits, and she let him take her hand as they meandered between haystacks that looked like miniature mountains in the moonlight.

"Let's climb up this one," she said. "Just for a few minutes."

"Wait till you hear my idea," he said, clambering up beside her.

"You know," she said, when they were sitting next to one another, "here in the moonlight on this night in this moment, you look like William Holden."

"With this nose?"

"Stop it. What's your big idea?"

"I'll try to get a job with Hallmark cards in Kansas City and become a real American writer, write things that people who admire Norman Rockwell and Frank Sinatra's songs can read with understanding and pleasure. Not that *Id*-stuff, but 'I'll meet you in my dreams' kinds of things; and then we could rendezvous from time to time. My old college roommate's the CEO."

"Spend an evening now and then spooning under a willow tree in the bottom land behind the Little House on the Prairie?"

"Why not?" he said. "It would be something."

"And, what? You would write immortal Chinese Fortune Cookie words like . . . *Age is relative . . . Everything is relative except one's relatives . . .*"

"Not bad, I've actually thought of that."

"Be serious."

"You know what?"

"I'm afraid to ask."

"In this moonlight on this night, you remind me of Rose of Sharon at the very end of *Grapes of Wrath*."

"Give me a break."

"No, really. At this moment . . . you and I really don't belong anywhere. If we say goodbye forever, we've lost the chance of a lifetime. You wouldn't have to give up anything, and I'd have something."

"An improbable meeting on a lonely planet."

"Something like that: an enlightened hayseed and a disenchanted *Hasid*," he said.

"Funny," she said, "but this isn't a Malamud story."

"See? You know something about the cultural pickle barrel. Will you think about it? No rush. I have to finish the term and see if my old roommate can find a slot for me. You don't have to burn any bridges."

"Not many wooden ones in Kansas, but just thinking about it makes me nervous. Still, I can't say I haven't wanted to escape, to flee, to see the bright lights again . . . but it's crazy to go on like this."

"It's not crazy, you've just been in denial too long."

"Back to the Id, I see," she said. "You've been in the East too long, too many hours on the couch."

"I couldn't agree more, and maybe you've been in the West too long."

"It's possible."

"Let's leave it there for the moment, we can talk about it more tomorrow."

"And if I'm not here?"

"We'll write, e-mail, do FaceTime . . . just thinking that something between us may be possible changes everything for both of us, at least for a while."

She scanned the sky and took a deep breath, "You're a schemer and a dreamer, but come closer."

"How much closer can I get?"

"Here," she said. "Here." Slowly, button by button, hesitating as she fumbled with the last one, opening her blouse and baring herself to him. "Here, tomorrow is another day. I don't want you depending on the kindness of strangers."

He moved closer and thought of *The Great Gatsby*—the "secret place above the trees," the big "gulp," "the tuning fork that had been struck upon a star. . . ." It was more thrilling to Ludwig than the overture to *Oklahoma,* but he knew the moment couldn't last. They were above the ground and would have to climb down, but a bond had been formed between them. If nothing else, the thought of her giving herself to him on this haystack would get him through some lonely hours in the nights ahead.

After a few quiet minutes, they walked silently, hand in hand, back towards the Moonglow. He lingered expectantly, eagerly, at the door of her room. She hesitated and leaned her head against his shoulder, kissed him lightly on the cheek, put the key in the door, and said, "Not now, not now."

"When?" he asked. "Where?" But she was already inside.

He waited outside her door for a few seconds, thought he heard her crying, and then, helpless to do anything, walked out to the edge of the field and lay down, pressing his nose into the wet grass. The earth smelled like champagne to him, and he savored its bouquet.

He inhaled the aromatic loam and felt like a somewhat different person, even as he didn't know how long the feeling would last. Only time would tell, but he was prepared to wait. He had no other option at this point in his life, but at least there might . . . just might . . . be this option.

And hadn't his grandfather Jacob sailed into a dream when he arrived in New York Harbor in 1906? Jacob had wandered into the future. Now Ludwig wondered about it. Something might be possible. He remembered what his father had said to him, even after the collapse of the gabardine market: "Never say it's the last road, the end of the way. You never know when a blue bolt will turn up and you can maybe make a coat." Well, there had been a bolt from the blue, sort of.

Then he heard himself humming, "And now when there's moonglow . . . way up in the blue . . . I always remember that moonglow gave me you. . . ."

The Icicles of Eggertsville

Mount Murray is a hill in the Catskill Range. A Yiddish expression is carved on a large stone at its peak: "A tserisn gemit iz shver tsum heyln." (A wounded spirit is hard to heal.) No one knows how it got there.

It had begun quietly, but quickly, in late October among noisy teenagers giggling over selfies at Starbucks and ended abruptly a year later in silence at a sushi restaurant, but it had ended, and he couldn't put the blame on edamame.

Although he wasn't a three-star Michelin gourmet, loss was one of Ludwig Fried's *spécialités de la maison*. He had spent decades trying to figure out—during the long Buffalo winters, when icicles the length of cathedral organ pipes hung on the eaves like stalactites—why life had served this dish to him, or why he had prepared it in ways that he didn't understand.

He had known, of course, as a veteran of many therapeutic campaigns and many romantic defeats, that he would be eligible for a *croix de crotch*, if there were one. But he couldn't find the whole recipe, only some of the ingredients, and he knew the metaphor wasn't very useful in any case.

Still, he was familiar with some of the ingredients, and each romantic failure had given him an opportunity to find another one, if only he faced unpleasant facts and told himself the truth, never easy for anyone.

Of course, truth itself was an elusive concept and its origins were rooted in the fog of childhood and the labyrinth of the brain's structure, so maybe there was no way for him out of the maze of aloneness that he so often found himself lost in. Maybe it just was the human condition.

In fact, he once built a small maze in his own garden to practice getting out of his existential puzzle, except it had been too small to get into. But as a dedicated gardener and perpetual memoirist, he wasn't about to turn in his trowel and give up digging.

He was in the twilight of his life, but twilight lingered during the summer in Western New York. Not Lapland, Buffalo seemed sometimes to be on the rim of the arctic circle, especially in winter, and these long summer twilights gave him hope with breezes fluttering off Lake Erie that stirred the long and graceful branches of his blue spruce, branches like elephant ears, evidence that there was movement in the world.

And now that he had a small deck where he could perch, as if he were in the crow's nest of a New Bedford whaler. He could hear the rich at play who lived beyond the blue spruce and over a chain-link fence: the *pock* of tennis balls, the plash of children in azure-tile lined pools, chatter about the rise and fall of the Dow as if it were the Roman Empire.

Hemingway loved the words "beyond" and "over." They created space for the mind to hunt in. Ludwig was no Hem, but he loved the literary bull's words, and once had laid a pine branch on Papa's grave in Ketchum, Idaho. Now he would reread some of the hunter's stories and see if they could help him get beyond and over a recent emotional wound, the *cojones* of the heart.

Now that he had a lookout, it made him feel as if he were at the wheel of a 16th century Portuguese caravel and could look back at his life through a spy-glass with a measure of objectivity, or so he thought. He might discover some previously hidden new worlds. It always was a question of *so he thought*, he thought.

But what was the alternative? If Ronald Reagan had been the "great communicator," Ludwig Fried was the "great ruminator," at least on his modest street where his neighbors *really* worked for a living. As he often said, chortling, one of his tics, where he "worked in quotes."

He lived in Eggertsville, Buffalo's nearest suburb, circa 1950. He had seen "Eggert," the road, but not the "ville." If it ever had existed, it had been paved over like a repressed memory. One would have to be an urban archeologist to find what might have been a coach stop in 1820 when Western New York was the leading edge of the expanding frontier, to the west even of James Fennimore Cooper territory.

And he would have to be an introspective navigator, a Prince Irving the Navigator of the inner map, if he was going to figure out why and how he had managed to end up--he searched for the right and true words--*alone on his deck.*

How had he managed to watch icicles as big as the Ritz lengthen during the long winter nights without a sympathetic companion by his side to warm his spirits? What had he done to make Rita, his *señorita* from Malibu, cut the cord six months ago that bound them umbilically together, or so he had thought?

The story of his failure, hers, theirs, no one's, was worth a book in itself. It was a job for a poet, as Sherwood Anderson had said in "Hands," and though Ludwig was an ex-bard, he still would give it the old college try, as they used to say in the pre-Viet Nam era, before a new generation had said kaddish for the Ivy League rah-rah spirit.

The writer's muse could be a real bitch, especially the Israeli beauty, Delilah, a visiting assistant professor of Diasporic Studies, who had left him in a ditch many years ago when she hooked up with an editor at *The Daily Forward* after he accepted one of her articles, "Shrunken Lives in the American Diaspora."

She certainly had cut Ludwig down to size—so much so that he found himself checking his pecker at random moments to make sure his dingle was still dangling. Wounded, he still would try to make sense of the past and then write about all the places he and Rita had planned to go together and where they were when they made their plans, places they now would not see as a couple trekking the lonely planet, a future that never would become their present.

Their future had quickly become a ruin in the past like the Catskill resort of his adolescence when he had worked as a boat-boy at Scaroon Manor on Schroon Lake, an upper notch on the Borscht Belt in the lower Adirondacks. If the timbers of the faux log cabins of Grossinger's the Concord, and Scaroon Manor could be repurposed as planks for Hasidic Sukkot huts, it might be possible for Ludwig the Inquisitor to put himself on trial in an effort to salvage some splinters and spars from his recent shipwreck on the shoals of a sushi bar.

If he was mixing metaphors, he chortled, it only made sense because he had been mixed-up for most of his life. If his psyche was Grand Central Station, few trains ever reached Greenwich without being derailed.

But this was private knowledge.

He hadn't been such a big *shnuck*, or worse, a *shmuck*, however, to let his former colleagues see his ship foundering as he seemed to be sailing through the halls of the department, his sheets puffed with the wind of small, but reputable, publications.

How did the end begin? What did he know and when did he know it? It's Watergate all over again, he chuckled, or maybe *The Education of Ludwig Fried.*

Like Henry Adams's alter ego, "Israel Cohen," Ludwig had been "handicapped" or self-handcuffed by his history.

Now was an op to find out why and how he-she-they had failed to canter into the sunset together. He was ready to ruminate as he sat on his deck, a glass of kosher *Lower Golan Prosecco* in one hand, a fine-tipped uni-ball Vision pen, *his* 6.5 Mannlicher, in the other.

The taxi to take him to the Buffalo airport for his flight to JFK and then El Al to Tel Aviv, where his daughter lived, wouldn't come until 6.30 a.m., and he was packed, socks rolled like bullets in a six-shooter. He had all night to weave together the rent fabric of the past like the shawl he had bought for Rita at the Carmel Market, not knowing that it, and their relationship, was rent goods.

He wasn't sure it could be stitched together. No tailor like his grandfather, no garment center manufacturer like his father, Ludwig nonetheless had inherited some of the instincts of the needle trades. At the end of the day, words and phrases weren't so different from swatches and end-pieces. Something could be made of them if you weren't into bespoke tailoring like Henry James.

His father had shipped to Sears and J.C. Penny, so Ludwig had written fiction for women's magazines, an occasional essay on cultural fashion in *Women's Wear Daily*, and a few articles on the lost American writers of the 1920s, enough to get him tenure at a small college on the outskirts of Buffalo, but not enough to retire as a full professor. He had been true to himself, a mixed blessing.

Well, he had made a life and things began to look up when Rita tripped at Starbuck's that fall afternoon and he had caught her smartphone. She couldn't have been more grateful if he were Sir Lancelot, so she invited him outside to chat.

She knew more about social media than he did about Shakespeare, so it was easy for him, at a loss in the electronic world, to ask questions, and she, Quaker-Buddhist-social worker, was impressed by how selfless he seemed to be, how eager he was to learn. She knew he was chatting her up, but she liked the style of his pitch. You could judge a man by the quality of his come-on, and she had been alone for too long with her thoughts of the tragic mystery.

They texted one another for a week in which he pecked out his wit and she said that the wattage of her inner light had glowed more brightly since the meeting at Starbuck's had brought them together.

Both adults, she sixty, he seventy, it had taken only one-day trip a week later to a winery along the southern shore of Lake Ontario for them to get together under the Amish quilts in her spacious country house on the outskirts of Buffalo where the deer roamed, an 1880s farmhouse that reminded him of the cottage in Austria where Hemingway had written *The Sun Also Rises*. Maybe Rita could be his Hadley.

They seemed quickly to fit. She liked clever men. Her late husband Cliff had been an astrophysicist, mountain climber, and a Los Angeles County champion Scrabble player, and when Ludwig said he "preferred quilts to guilt," she had been charmed.

"I think we might have a lot to talk about," she said. "I'd like to find some nice spots for a conversation."

That "might" should have made him wary, but he wanted to get closer to her and half-believed he could woo her away from the past with words. He would try to fit into her life, even if it meant, with his L-5 stenosis, limping along the shores of Lake Ontario.

"Do you know Golden Hill State Park?" she said. "It's empty this time of year. There's even a lighthouse there."

"I'll try to go with you to as many places as possible," he said, without adding that he'd be limping most of the time. He would try to walk the walk and talk the talk so he could get to the underwater floor of a relationship with her. "Towards" and "trying" were keywords for Ludwig, and many of his exes—more than filled a tic-tac-toe box—had found his quest for a shared seabed to be a burden.

"Too needy" had been the pink slip at the end of more than a few trysts, especially with the women who were themselves questing souls, who didn't want to be tethered to a man's desires. And Rita had made it clear that first night that she was searching for "summit beyond suffering, an eternal present." She liked having him in her bed with winter coming on, but she needed to be alone, finally, where she depended on no one and no one depended on her.

"Good," she said. "We can make a list of all the places we'd like to see together. It can be our game."

They would have had a better chance of making it together, he now realized, if they had been Canadian geese, paired for life, but he had taken the plunge that night with only a moment's hesitation.

And they really did seem to fit. It was, he whispered to her, after their first caress, as if two missing adjoining pieces of a jigsaw puzzle had turned up. A lover of board games, she was delighted by the image.

"Cliff loved board games before he," she hesitated, "disappeared."

"Disappeared?" Ludwig asked, gently.

"Too deep to go into now," she said. "But my husband went missing at Mount Abu ten years ago, at the Indian Astronomical Observatory in the Himalayas, highest one in the world."

"I'm sorry," he said.

She didn't say anything at first, but snuggled more tightly, as if the crevice between them needed to be closed.

"I'm trying to get over it, it's difficult. We had no children, his childhood had been too painful, his father was a suicide, we just had each other," she said. Then added, "But he was doing what he needed to do. He went to the highest places so he could look the farthest into the universe, but something went wrong. They're still looking for him."

"I know about searching," he said. "I've been seeing a shrink for years, spelunking in the unconscious."

"And he was a great scrabble word," she said, pressing closer. "I used to love the game, but after Cliff disappeared, I began to meditate. I need to find a place in the universe where I belong."

"The cosmos?"

"Something like that. Aren't we made of the same particles? The universe is still a mystery."

"Like the brain," he said, trying to bring her closer to his mental library. "It seems to be as complicated as the universe."

If she looked to Carl Sagan for meaning, he had found more, at least in his youth, in Francois Sagan, but he buttoned his lip. After all, he had learned something about buttons in the garment center from his father whose father had sold "old clothes" off a pushcart on Canal Street.

"I keep searching for that inner Shangri-la. I mediate every morning at dawn. I keep searching for the right mantra, the one that will put me in touch with the music of the spheres. Sometimes I hum and chant, listening for the right harmony."

"I should go home then and let you sleep."

"No, you can sleep as long as you want, it's a weekend, I'll have breakfast when you wake up. I'm glad you're here. It helps. I need to move on."

Looking back, he knew he should have left at that point. She wasn't likely to find him in a movie version of *Lost Horizon*. He was no Ronald Coleman.

But if they spent enough time together in all the places they both wanted to see in which they could learn more about each other, he hoped that she could accept the coat they were stitching together from the end-pieces of their lives.

He thought of Pascal. If Rita could give up her quest for the "infinitely large," she might accept him as the "infinitely small," but no *schlemiel*. If he couldn't be an Adirondack peak, he was, at least, Mt. Murray where he had worked as a boat-boy one summer in the upper Catskills.

And because they fit together so tightly and gracefully that night, leaving would have felt like emotional hara-kiri. She felt it, too, at least at first, he had hoped.

"Look," she said, their entwined arms casting a shadow on the oak panels of her bedroom, "we could be mistaken for strands of kelp."

"Maybe we can kelp each other."

"I hope so," she said, laughing and then curving the arch of her foot against his leg. "See, we're like two shells, one resting in the other, a coral reef."

He wanted to think that they might meet in the deep sea vents of a late middle age relationship. After all, they were partners in loss, she as the result of a tragic enigma and he, long divorced, the father of an only child who had decided to make a new life in a new old land, Israel, *Erertz* for her.

"We can visit some of the places that inspired me," he said, matching his fingers with Rita's. "And you can show me some of the landscapes that lifted your spirits. We'll learn from each other."

"For example?"

"Mt. Rushmore."

"Not until they carve a woman president," she said.

"And you?"

"San Miguel de Allende."

"Mexico?" he asked.

"Yes. My father took us there after the war. He wanted to write a novel about his traumatic experience, the men who were lost in his bomber squadron. You could live on the cheap there, and he had the G.I. Bill. Your turn."

"Don't rush, I don't want to use up all my geographical tiles. Which reminds me, I can show you the mosaics at Zippori."

"Where is that?"

"Israel, it's like the seven layers of Troy."

"One more, please, I like this game."

Ludwig's heart beat faster. He had begun to think, even believe, that Rita might want to trot into the future with him.

"How about Cascais?"

"Where in Emerson's name is that?"

"Emerson?"

"I'm part Unitarian," she said. "Where is Cascais?"

"On the Tagus River, ten miles from Lisbon, where the estuary meets the sea. I saw it when I took a year off from college and backpacked across Europe. I met Hemingway in Paris that year. I'd like to show you some of the places that I'd still like to write about and the things that happened there."

"Tell me more."

"Just one more. Key West, you'd like that, Hemingway lived there. The Ithaca bitch and I had the 'good destruction' there before she totaled me. Eventually we can go to Cuba. It's bound to open up one of these days. But you really need to sleep."

"You're right," she said, turning away slightly, but pulling his arm around her waist as if she were a mountain climber and needed a safety line. He was pleased to be one, at least for a while, if that's what she needed him to be, if that's what it would take for them to live together more fully in the present.

A harvest moon, as vivid as an Ansel Adams photograph, cast a glow over them and he thought of Kim Novak and William Holden dancing to the tune of "Moonglow" in *Picnic*. He and Rita weren't as young and attractive, but he was something of a drifter, and they had come together as lonely strangers at Starbucks--*strangers in the night*--the subject of his only published article, but a "citation classic," the one that had gotten him his tenure. It had made a small dent in the fender of the academic world.

As he drifted into sleep, he dreamed about what he came to call his billiard ball theory of anxiety, his only attempt at a scientific model of experience. Each large Daliesque ball represented, as he came to decipher it later, a romantic avalanche in which he had been buried.

As he was about to run out of air to breathe, another ball rolled along and knocked the first one into a pocket, just as Rita seemed to be someone who might knock off the green felt and into the pocket the last woman in his life with whom the Velcro of intimacy had failed to hold—the origin of which failure was as baffling to him as the quest for the origin of life itself. Maybe birth was the problem.

Montaigne had asked, "What do I know?" ("Que sais-je?"), and had come up with a few essays. Like Ludwig, he probably wouldn't have gotten tenure at a major university, but, lucky for him, he was a landed aristocrat and could retreat to his library tower in Guyenne outside of Bordeaux.

As Ludwig snuggled close to Rita on many cold Buffalo winter nights with snowdrifts like white elephants surrounding her house, he thought that her bed might become like the tower in which Michel Eyquem de Montaigne had written his famous essays, his gift of the "I" to the world.

The comparison wasn't crazy. After all, Montaigne's great-grandfather, Ramon, had been a herring merchant and his maternal grandfather, Pedro Lopez, from Zaragoza, descended from a wealthy Portuguese family.

Ludwig's paternal grandfather, Otto from Zbecno, had sold "old pickles." One of his sons had made a fortune manufacturing brassieres, and Ludwig had written many personal *feuilletons*, as he liked to call them.

But now was the time to live, not write, up close and personal. He heard a fragment of a phrase whose origin he couldn't name … *live ... live all you can.* When the time was right, he would read Martin Buber's *I and Thou* and Rilke's *Letters to a Young Poet* to Rita. Nothing would bring them closer together than to be on the same page under the same sheets together. As a great college professor once told him between puffs of his meerschaum, "Life creates possibilities for literature, literature creates possibilities for life." If Ludwig had a mantra, that was it. He wondered about hers.

As winter deepened and they played more place-games with each other after uncertain love-making, uncertain that he was letting him deeply into her life, he began to gain a jot and title of confidence that he and Rita were a couple who had rescued each other from solitude.

But he wasn't sure that she had found the inner harmony that would make that possible. It occurred to him one night that it might make a good board game. Each question could be a card that might land them on *Too Alone to Fail.*

"What place would you most like to see together?" he asked one night.

"That's a tough one. Maybe Lantau Island, just a few miles from Hong Kong in the South China Sea. There's a Buddhist temple at the top of a small mountain. My father said he found some peace there after the war."

"And you? What would you most like us to see together?"

"Talk about tough. Maybe Terengganu, an island off the East Coast of Malaysia. I went snorkeling there one moonlit night along a coral reef. I never felt so connected to life. Sounds lame, I know, but I don't know how else to say it. Or maybe Mt. Hermon in Israel. You can see Lebanon and Syria from its upper ridges. It all looks like one peaceful land at that height. One snowfall is general over all the region."

"Connection is everything," she said as she eased into sleep.

When she slipped out of bed that night, he pretended to be asleep, but he wanted to know somehow if her meditation was helping her get closer to the place where she wanted to be. Her breathing and humming, her words, if audible, might be a key. He would be a spy in the camp of her inner life. It might tell him what move to make next.

He waited a few minutes and tiptoed towards her meditation room at the top of the stairs. She kept her back to the door, so she didn't notice him peering in. She sat cross-legged in front of a small statue of the Buddha, rosy-cheeked children clinging to him, at whose sides two joss sticks glowed slightly in the pre-dawn light. A sandalwood-framed photograph was placed evenly above the porcelain statue. Ludwig listened carefully, but couldn't make out any words. She seemed to be murmuring something haltingly, but it might have been only uneven breathing, and he couldn't make out the figure in the faintly visible photograph that seemed to be standing on a snowcapped mountain. Or maybe it was the Taj Mahal. He couldn't be sure. Something white seemed to be gleaming.

He leaned toward the opening in the door and held his own breath so he could make out more clearly what she was saying, if she was uttering words. In the quiet of his inner ear, he thought he heard her weeping as she looked up at the photograph and extended her arms in what seemed to be a beckoning and welcoming gesture, like Gatsby staring at the green light across the harbor.

He thought of the lonely times after Delilah had pink-slipped him, when he had stood at the end of Anglin's Pier in Lauderdale-by-the-Sea during the period of his visits to his parents during the years of their exile in Florida.

Watching Princess Line cruise ships ease their way out of Port Everglades as they headed towards the Caribbean, he had felt stuck at the red traffic light of his life. But then, so many years later, he and Rita had become, he thought, Starbucked lovers and would sail the Seven Seas together.

Not to be, he thought, as her weeping became somewhat more audible, *I can't fill the gap in her life, we'll never travel together. I'll never see those places that I wanted to write about. Goodbye Vasco de Gama, hello Prince Irving the Navigator of the inner map.*

He knew in this instant that he wouldn't have to see a shrink to learn that his life was on the verge of being diminished again. If he had been a sub-atomic particle on the verge of the Big Bang, he just might end up being one of the "-ons." Not a moron, but small nonetheless.

There was no way to pre-shrink hope, and he had gone for the bait again like a fish suckered by a lure.

He had seen tropical fish lose their iridescence in a flash when hooked and left flapping on Anglin's pier. Ludwig remembered Hemingway's nasty and dismissive description of Dos Passos: "White as the under half of an unsold flounder at 11 o'clock in the morning."

Still, he felt a surge of empathy for Rita in this moment and began to step into her room to comfort her. She, sensing him, turned around suddenly.

"You should be sleeping, not invading my space," she almost shouted.

Embarrassed, at a loss for words, and reduced to a stammer, he stepped quickly back and found himself sliding down the carpeted staircase whose thick nap cushioned his descent.

Panicked that he might not live to add another publication to his slim bibliography, he managed to protect his head by rolling himself somehow into a ball as if he were a pink *Spaldeen* from the schoolyard of his New York City childhood and bounced into the laundry basket that Rita had put at the bottom of the staircase before they went to bed.

"Oh, my god, oh, my god." He heard her scream as he was engulfed in sheets that bore the scent of their lovemaking. She rushed down the stairs and did her best to pull him out of the snowfield of white linen in which he seemed to be buried.

"It's okay," he said. "I think I can stand."

"I thought I had lost you. I wasn't sure I'd be able to talk to you again."

"It's okay. I don't think I broke anything. I didn't lose my footing on Kilimanjaro."

She reached out to help him up.

"I can't forget what might have happened," she said almost inaudibly.

"I know," he said, after a long pause. "I've known it for some time, but I kept hoping."

"We can still travel together, you can still write about what we see together," she said as she wrapped her arms around him protectively.

"I appreciate that. We'll see what we can work out. It may take some time."

"You make us some coffee, I'll finish my meditation and join you."

Those were the last words they exchanged.

He managed to get upstairs to dress and then to descend quietly without disturbing her inner journey to get to a higher place beyond suffering.

* * *

An Urgent Care Ambulance stopped at the house across the street where the recluse lived. Ludwig had tried to befriend him from to time, but it had been hopeless. He always knew that when he became the "lonely guy," as the kids left the house, this is the way he would leave.

The flashing lights of the ambulance snapped Ludwig out of his deep rumination. He checked his watch: 3 a.m. The taxi would come in a few hours to take him to the airport. He needed to get some sleep if he didn't want to look like Frankenstein when he arrived in Israel.

Ludwig felt strangely calm and taut, like an Olympic sprinter poised at the starting block waiting for the gun to fire. He was ready to begin his trip to see and write about all those places they had mentioned as they played their night-games.

I may have fallen into the laundry basket, he thought, *but I'm no basket case.*

He felt a surge of energy. Rita had reduced the globe of his future into a ball—what he had hoped would be *their* world—but now he was ready to expand. There was so much to see and write about that their tender, fragile, and doomed relationship had made possible.

He wouldn't know for some time if he was a loser or a winner.

He could barely wait to leave. It would feel like a life-time before the taxi came, but it would come. It always had come on time before, and there was no reason why it wouldn't come on time this time. It was a good company.

Second Time Around

"So glad we met the second time around . . ."

Ten miles north of Lockport, NY, Ludwig Fried, connoisseur of uncertainty, sat, near twilight, middle of May, semi-slumped in a sun-tracking chair on his small pine deck that overlooked Lake Ontario. The swirls and curlicues in the still-glistening grain of the wood reminded him of inner worlds and distant galaxies.

Imagining that he was in the crow's nest of a 19th century Portuguese caravel, he liked to pretend that he was setting sail for some of the faraway places he still wanted to see and write about: Keats's Hampstead Heath cottage, Tolstoy's Yasnaya Polyana estate, "the old Moulmein Pagoda."

But he wasn't sure if it made sense at his age and stage of life to voyage out. For better and worse, wasn't his life as complete as it could be? What could he find out there that he hadn't already found?

A retired Lecturer of Composition and Memoir Writing, Niagara County Community College, "mini-man of letters," as he thought of himself when low, "mildly successful" when upbeat, he scanned the horizon line and arc of Lake Ontario from west to east.

He could see the Canadian shoreline curving towards Hamilton and Toronto, the CNN Tower, visible on this clear evening, and the pulsating beam of the Thirty Point Lighthouse only fifteen miles down Lake Ontario Road. His perch gave him a sense of belonging to a larger world than the one in which he lived mainly by himself.

"*You call that living, the asshole of Canada?*" he heard his late father say.

"*But it's not Canada, pop, it's America.*"

"*So what? It's still an asshole.*"

Long divorced, many friends retired to Arizona, California, and Taos—recent lady friend unable to overcome her grief for a husband, MIA, Viet Nam; brother, retired dentist, Boca; daughter and grandchildren, Israel—he found himself more or less alone. Maybe the human condition, but definitely his.

Not so uncommon at his age and stage of life for many of his contemporaries, privileged rebels, who had resisted living life as usual in the 1960s, but, again, it was *his* life. Statistics and demographics didn't help when Daylight Savings Time ended and he felt on the verge of entering a darkening world.

Grandson of Czech exiles, tending to look at life more through the shadowy lens of Prague's Franz Kafka than the Brooklyn bifocals of Hasidic rabbis who found light and joy even in the shadows and dark corners of the world, he was grateful now for the expanse of vision and the perspective it encouraged.

Not about to give in to the forces of introspective entropy, he still sometimes thought that the human race was a flawed species living on an endangered planet in a universe destined, according to his secular bible, *The New York*

Times, for extinction. But it was more a mood than a conviction.

He was especially grateful for the panoramic view on this evening when he needed to make a decision. Should he or shouldn't he accept Archy Fine's wedding invitation just a month away on the cusp of the summer solstice? Not "to be or not to be," but important to Ludwig, for whom all irreversible decisions seemed to be a step towards the gallows.

The ceremony would take place only a few miles away in one of Midsummer Winery's secluded organic apple orchards, heritage acreage, not far from where Archy's surprisingly younger bride-to-be, Francine, had spent summers in her family's opulent lakeside estate.

Improbably and unexpectedly, old Arch, fingers gnarled, long-divorced veteran of serial romances with former artsy students, would tie the knot with Francine Chapin, Bennington graduate, Freudian, film historian (Eastman House, Rochester), only child, estranged from her socially snobbish parents, owners of a golf course.

Francine—scholar, free spirit, agile body, accepting of his uncertain Viagra-assisted amatory overtures—had put a bounce in his step, he reported, a Sousa-like rhythm after some years of just *schlepping* along: "Got lucky at an Elder Hostel in Taos where Francine was lecturing on 'D.H. Lawrence's Cinematic Vision: Sexuality and Rebirth.'"

Archy, distinguished Chaucer scholar, former Dean of Humanities, Bard College, now living in a condo off Lexington Avenue, had been one of Ludwig's great roommates at Columbia during the "silent generation" where they had spent many late hours on the cusp of the Ginsburg and Kerouac generation discussing their futures at the fabled West End Bar.

Arch, valedictorian, Bronx Science, 160 IQ, had been confident that he would climb the academic ladder, while Ludwig, prone to slipping, was uncertain if he could find a voice that would link stand-up comedy and Henry James, the poles of his quirky imagination:

Lamb House and the Catskills.

"It's risky, Lud, very risky, late in the day for another Jewish American writer, stick to criticism, that's the path to tenure."

The wedding itself wasn't the problem, as dicey a January-May arrangement as it seemed to be on the face of things. The guests who would attend were the cause of his *angst*. For Ludwig, anxiety came with a German accent.

Helen Fine, Archy's first wife, now a Buddhist and Quaker, committed to "higher truths," as Archy had reported, "eager, dear soul, in the spirit of cosmic harmony, to forgive you for your early devotion to a career, not me," retired Curator of Sacred Books, St. Bonaventure University, New York's Southern Tier.

Daniel Blum, Greenwich Village Marxist, French wine expert, Professor of English (Vassar), author of a brilliant article, a citation classic, "Being Right on the Left Bank," and a four decade old work in progress—*Adorno and Adon Alom: Crisis in the Bronx*.

Robert Greensward, well-known postmodern and experimental poet, author of a cult volume, *Enameled Frost*, Don Juan, barely getting by on social security in a rent controlled apartment in Brooklyn Heights and long-term residences at artist colonies, Yaddo, MacDowell, always on the lookout for a live-in possibility with a patron of the arts who had an adequate trust fund and ample bosom.

Tiffany Printz, daughter of two Bronx-born Munich trained Park Avenue psychoanalysts, writer, shapely implants, whose biographies of closeted Hollywood lesbians had made her wealthy, to say nothing of an inherited International Style beach house on Provincetown Bay with wraparound windows and a teak deck.

He hadn't seen any of them for many years. Out of mind most of the time, they were often present in Ludwig's recurring dream of having his short fiction rejected by this "editorial board" who had attended Archy's first wedding.

The old wedding had been a pastoral affair on Chautauqua Lake, service presided over by a "bi-curious" Unitarian Universalist Minister who read passages from Emerson's essay on "Circles" and *Leaves of Grass*.

A little over the top, looking back to the apocalyptic 1960s, but pleasant enough to recall. Still, did it make sense for Ludwig, a minor-league Gatsby, to revisit the past? Archy had "invited all the stars, the old crowd." None of them had lost their imposing presence in Ludwig's mental firmament.

Archy had written: "The service will be held near Golden Hill State Park, your neck of the woods, not far from where Francine took her first Martha Graham-style ballet lessons, Lockport. I'm just inviting the old crowd. Francine wants to know my ancient history. We'll send announcements to everyone else. Maybe have a larger celebration later."

All graduate students in English at Princeton at the time of the first wedding, except for Ludwig when he was working in the mailroom at Doubleday & Co. and collecting rejection slips, the old crowd had made him feel like an outsider, marginal.

They hadn't exactly looked down on him in any obvious or intentional way on that weekend, and maybe they were just avoiding a delicate subject, but none of them had made him feel that he would make it as a writer.

"*And you haven't, big shot,*" he heard his father say, "*give me a break, whoever heard of The Catskill Quarterly, give me Women's Wear Daily.*"

Like Arch, they had known that it was safer to have a Ph.D. from an Ivy League graduate school than a pile of rejection slips and some acceptances from obscure journals if you wanted to make a living as a literary person in America during the dull Eisenhower years.

If they hadn't thought of him then as a loser, they didn't want to encourage him to become one.

They all seemed to be going up the academic escalator while he was going down at the time of the first nuptial and the few years after when they would come into Manhattan on weekends and exchange clever banter at The Princeton Club bar. Alexander, the bartender, distantly related to the Romanovs, always put an extra olive in *their* martinis and asked him if he wanted a bottle of BUD.

They would talk about the job offers that were coming in over the transom while all he could report was another rejection slip from *Commentary*, *The Partisan Review,* and obscure magazines in Ohio and Oklahoma. In those days, they seemed like Dom Perignon to his Manischewitz. If he thought they might be saying a *Kiddush* for him then, he was worried it might be *Kaddish* this time.

If he attended the wedding, the old feelings might return. He had spent years in a garden variety of psychotherapies trying to disentangle the past and the present, but he hadn't been a successful patient.

"*Customer! You're paying through the schnozola, forget this patient crap!*"

As his father had failed in the low overhead garment business, busted when America shifted from gabardine *shmattes* to synthetics, so Ludwig had been able to move the goods in those days only in the bargain basement of small magazines.

As his father had been plagued with "returns," Ludwig had been unable to overcome fully a history of rejection slips, even though he knew in rare moments of clarity on an evening such as this one that he had done as well as most minor writers in America.

After all, 95% of them who were featured in *Poets & Writers* were less well known than poor Joe Gould who had made only a few scrawled entries in some coffee-stained notebooks. Most MFA degrees stood for Minor Faculty Artist.

That word "minor" was Ludwig's Scarlet Letter, Achilles heel, psychological hernia, self-flagellating cat-o'-nine-tails, and he was afraid that meeting the Princeton crowd again would put him on the rack with his writer's balls in a vice and his ego in a Cuisinart, a whirring blunder.

And there would be no way to conceal the truth of the life he had lived. Archy had urged each of the featured guests to write out a brief biographical statement, in the form of a *desiderata*: "Let's catch up and get to know each other again in case we've forgotten how much we meant to one another, how special we were. Let's rekindle the old flame around a campfire."

If Archy thought they should act as if they were going to Canterbury and staying at the Tabard Inn, where they would regale each other with inspirational tales of brilliant Princeton evenings in Holder Hall, Ludwig wasn't sure he could take it.

They had been Edmund Wilson to his F. Scott Fitzgerald. Of course, they weren't Wilsons and he wasn't Scott or John Peale Bishop, but there was some emotional truth for him in the analogy, especially at three in the morning when he needed a shot of *Chivas Regal* to fall asleep.

"*Go, don't be a putz,*" he heard his father say, "*go, sell yourself, what are you, a bum?*"

His late father made sense some of the time. If he didn't attend the wedding, he never would know if he had managed to come to terms with what his life had added up to. In fact, he wouldn't know what it had added up to if he didn't meet the old crowd, an exclusive eating club who sometimes had a *nosh* in his unconscious and occasionally woke him in the middle of the night and made him feel that he had consigned himself to a life in the literary Gulag.

But he would come late, keep his distance, test the waters, and he always could leave. But he couldn't insult Archy, boon companion of his Manhattan youth, and, given where Ludwig lived, the nearby town of Wilson on the Lake, he would have to come up with a lame medical excuse not to attend.

He also owed something to Dr. Ernst Lichtenstein, his personal trainer of the mind for so many years, whose last words to him had been, "As Goethe says, 'To thine own creativity be true.'"

He couldn't go against Dr. Lichtenstein and Goethe, but he didn't have to punish himself. He had been to enough prizefights in the old Madison Square Garden with his father to know how to feint and jab, if it came to that. He would duck, spar, and leave the ring if anyone tried to hit him below the emotional belt.

"That's my boy, remember Al Singer? He taught you how to throw a punch!"

He did remember Al: washed up, alcoholic, had thrown a fight in 1931, ruined his life. Ludwig's father, Al's childhood friend from their Mott Street days, had kept Al on the payroll as long as he could.

"Never take a dive, kid, remember Al."

At least he had a month to work on his *desiderata* once he found out exactly what it was. Having a vague idea that it was written by John Donne, it came as a relief somehow to learn that it wasn't penned with a quill by a major 17th century poet, but a forgotten American versifier, Max Ehrmann (1872-1945).

Max had been born in Terre Haute, Indiana, not Cambridge or Oxford, so Ludwig felt a little more at ease about going up against a poet whose one poem was as famous as Frost's "The Road Not Taken," but whose work wasn't included in *The Norton Anthology of American Literature*, a fate comparable to anonymity for an American writer.

"*You call that work?*" he heard his father say.

* * *

Ludwig walked slowly down a path through the apple orchard behind Midsummer Winery that led to a small hill overlooking the shore of Lake Ontario below which a *chuppah* had been erected on a freshly mown lawn. Pleased that he had arrived not a minute too soon, with evening coming on, he could slip away in the shadows like Red Grange, the Galloping Ghost, a childhood hero.

Archy, wearing blue jeans and a black cotton turtleneck, and Francine, in a white linen dress with festive opalescent Mexican embroidery, stood hand-in-hand beneath the *chuppah* to the side of which a string quartet of young Eastman School musicians were playing Samuel Barber's *Adagio for Strings*.

It seemed a bit doleful for the occasion, but then he could see that there was a poignant sadness about Francine. He could imagine her balletic movements as she moved solemnly through Pueblo ruins.

Only the old crowd sat in a row of Adirondack chairs in front of the *chuppah*, looking for all the world like the dignified dead in the last scene of *Our Town*. He scanned their lineaments as he stealthily approached and sat in a lone chair behind them.

He was surprised that he recognized the old crowd: Helen, Daniel, Bob, and Tiffany, all of them gray and stoop-shouldered. Daniel heavier than he had been, Bob slimmer, Helen gaunt, Tiffany subtly botoxed and face-lifted, they still were unmistakably themselves after all these years. He wondered how he would look to them since he seemed to see his father's worried post-bankruptcy face, brim of his fedora wrinkled, when he looked into the mirror these days.

He looked around to see who would officiate at the ceremony. No one who looked like a rabbi seemed to be present. Ludwig had been to some avant-garde weddings, but this one seemed a bit theatrical, a stage-set for an upbeat version of *No Exit*.

Archy stepped forward and gestured towards Ludwig, "Now that my old roomie is here, I knew he wouldn't stiff us, we can begin."

The Princeton quartet, not the musicians, turned around and nodded approvingly, it seemed, to acknowledge his presence, even to welcome him.

Archy continued, "Free spirits that we are, Francine and I have decided, in effect, if not in law, to marry ourselves. We'll be our own *officiants*, as they call them in traditional houses of worship. Veterans of the 1960s, battered, but not defeated, we're beyond tradition. And, by the way, we won't be singing any songs from *Fiddler on the Roof*."

"Right on, brother," Daniel shouted, raising a clenched left fist.

"Dead lyrics," Bob chimed in.

"Tevye's a bore, macho," Tiffany added.

"I knew I could count on you to raise the ceiling, Thomas Merton would approve," Helen said just above a whisper.

As if seeking his approval, they turned around to look at Ludwig.

"Yes, to thine own creativity be true, definitively," he added. The Princeton backfield, single wing, as he still thought of them, smiled at him whose students loved chicken wings.

Archy and Francine intertwined their fingers like a Hopi breadbasket and stepped forward.

Archy spoke first: "I, Archibald Fine, join you, Francine Chapin, the liberated spirit for whom I have been searching, lo, these many years, some of which have been, indeed, *low*, in a journey of body, mind, and spirit." He paused, smiled, looked at the old crowd, flashed a peace sign, and added, "I hope I haven't left anything out. If I have, you'll tell me around the campfire."

Francine disentangled her fingers and put her palms together Hindu style.

"*Shalom*, loyal members of Archy's ancient tribe. I, Francine Chapin, join Archibald Fine, the archetype of wisdom, no pun intended on this sacred occasion, as his partner in a journey to the peak of Mt. Parnassus."

As inspirited as their words seemed to be and as unlikely that their union really would work, Ludwig had to admit that he had said in earnest many more fanciful things to younger women in his Ponce de Leon quest for—he wasn't sure what to call it. That had been part of his problem—confusion.

None of the old crowd seemed perplexed. They were visibly moved by this improbable union of two such different—even contradictory—spirits. A set of opposite pairs, it occurred to him, they had moved closer to each other as Archy and Francine exchanged something like vows: Greensward leaning towards Tiffany, Helen edging closer to Daniel.

Some Goethean affinities seemed to be in the air.

Archy continued. "I promise to make every effort . . . at my age," he winked, "to become a member of Francine's tribe, to join her in a dance of life seven times, as tradition dictates, around her inner campfire . . . well, I did go to summer camp where the upper Catskills meet the lower Berkshires." He winked again.

Francine didn't so much smile as she glowed with the warmth of a spiritual satisfaction that coursed through her body.

"I promise to climb, to the extent that it is possible for me, to the summit of Archy's learning. After all, Bennington wasn't Princeton. I wore leotards; he donned, as it were, a scholar's robe, and really wore one at King's College later. In ourselves, we've been incomplete, but now . . . now . . . we hope . . . I think you know what I mean."

Both quartets, stirred, moved closer to each other. Violins neatly touching violas, a Marxist inching towards faith, a Park Avenue best-selling author, guilty about success, betrayed by aging, gravitating towards a poet who had been willing to pay the price, if not the rent, for his brilliant obscurity.

The string quartet finished the piece and walked quietly away just as the sun began to set over the Peace Bridge.

"Here's to us, all of us," Archy said as he and Francine stepped in unison on a ruby-red goblet, Bohemian cut-glass, wrapped in an embroidered white linen cloth.

Greensward spoke up, "Here's to deconstructed symbolism."

"And reconstructed lives," Tiffany said, putting her arm around him.

"Thesis and antithesis," Daniel added, as Helen gazed meditatively at him.

"Now join us for your *desiderata* and, of course, marshmallows," Archy said, taking Francine's hand and walking towards the slate-smooth shore where a campfire, catered, had been built for them.

"I'll let Lud enlighten us first," Archy said. "We need most to hear from him, he's been the most out of touch."

"*Show 'em what you're made of, kid, I've been waiting for this moment. Hit 'em in the kishkes, remember the Bronx cheer.*"

"I'll give it the old college try," Ludwig said.

"You can do it, Lud, I read one of your stories in the *Almost Dead-End Review* when I knew you might be here."

"Bob's right," Daniel said. "Me, too, that great monologue in 'Normie the Private,' you were marching with the masses when we were piling up footnotes instead of putting up barricades."

"Marginalia for me," Helen chimed in.

"Forbidden assignations with senior professors, love in the stacks, hidden lives, you were out there, Lud, we were cloistered, weren't we Daniel?"

"Tiff's right, Lud, you were on the front lines of history."

"But look where I ended up," Ludwig said, embarrassed by his frankness, gesturing towards the vast emptiness of Lake Ontario, no green light in sight.

"We all get lost, Lud," Archy said, hugging Francine, "it's what we learn that matters, the way out of the maze."

"Look at us," Francine said quietly, beaming at Archy.

The circle around the campfire tightened as they spoke. Helen and Daniel now seemed to be a couple as did Robert and Tiffany.

"We all get broken, kid, some get stronger in the broken places," he heard his father say. *"Amazing, pop, you've read Hemingway."*

"I had to do something in Florida, didn't I?"

"We're waiting for you, Lud," Archy said, adding some kindling to the fire, "you've kept your distance for too many years. Hasn't he?'

The Princeton quartet nodded.

"I'll be damned," Ludwig said.

"Aren't we all? Capitalist conspiracy," Daniel chimed in, half serious.

"Well, here goes," Ludwig said, "I hope no one is recording this, I don't want it to go viral."

"You should be so lucky."

They all smiled.

"I went unsure of myself among the literati and glitterati and found that I was greeted with silence. I tried, as far as possible, not to be envious or resentful . . . are you sure you want me to go on with this?"

They all nodded.

"I tried to speak the truth, to tell my story, even though it became clear that it wouldn't become a major motion picture . . . well, I never really believed that."

"I knew you had a bullshit detector!"

"Sounds familiar," Robert said.

"You're speaking for the masses, the silenced," Daniel added.

"Success can fuck you up," Tiffany said.

"I knew that there would be writers greater than I, but I tried not to think less of my work for all of that . . ."

"You were right to do so," Helen said quietly.

"I've tried to think well of my achievements, but I haven't always succeeded. . . ."

"You should have called, Lud," Archy said, some pain in his voice.

"Don't interrupt, Arch, we've had our say, he's speaking for the rest of us," Francine said. "Go on, Ludwig, please."

"My life hasn't been an origami. It hasn't unfolded as I hoped it would, I regret to say, so I came here with some reluctance. . . ."

"We needed you to come, Lud, you've spoken for all of us," Helen said. "More honestly than we would have spoken for ourselves. We've all lived incomplete lives, we're all serious losers, isn't that clear? That truth makes us closer, makes closeness possible, doesn't it?"

"Thanks, Helen."

"She's right, Lud, look at me, leisure of the theory class."

"You're looking at a footnote in someone's online literary history," Robert said.

"I tried to stop the clock, look at me, but not too closely," Tiffany said, voice lowered.

"And I had no children," Helen added.

"*The clock stops for everyone, Sonny, it's just a question of when, but you're still ticking.*"

"*Slowly, Pop, slowly.*"

"*But ticking.*"

"We're finally together after all these years," Archy said. "That's what's important."

"No need to read my *spiel*," Daniel said as he put a rolled sheet of paper in the fire. "Ludwig spoke for all of us."

One by one each added a scroll. The fire flared up, all the logs now glowed. With a prompt from Archy, they sang in unison an old camp song they all knew, "friends, friends, friends, we always shall be, whether in fair or dark stormy weather, by this lake our vows we make. . . ."

As a young couple paddled by in a canoe, feathered their oars and waved at them, the seven of them sang even louder and locked arms.

"*See, what did I tell you? Do I know my customers?*"

* * *

Looking back a few weeks later, Ludwig thought of the couple who had paddled by the improbable gathering of the once disparate and unified souls on that magical evening. It must have seemed to them, he imagined, that the group had stepped out of a painting by Breughel, Franz Halls, or Norman Rockwell—a living portrait that they might have called "A Merry Gathering of the Guild." They would have seen only the *joie de vivre*, no tincture of sadness, the spark of life, no flickering.

They might not all stay bonded, but they had fanned a dying ember in him and given him some hope that he, too, might now have enough confidence to go out into a larger world again and meet someone who might need him and whom he might need to make their lives more of a circle than a row of chairs.

"The odds are long, sonny."

He felt that he had been given, even seized, a second chance. The words of two favorite poems came back to him from his high school years—Tennyson's "Ulysses," Kipling's "Mandalay."

It was too late to "seek a newer world," and he didn't have enough medical coverage to go "somewhere east of Suez," but Archy's wedding, or something like a wedding, had shown him that even he, Ludwig Fried, ruminator, equivocator, floater, might be able to paddle away from the shoals of self-doubt and...

"Close the deal."

At that instant, he saw the beacon of the Thirty Mile Point Lighthouse sweep across the shoreline below his house.

"I told you, sonny, never take a dive! I made a come-back, didn't I? I left your mother a bundle."

If nothing else, it might be a story he could write and read to the wedding party when, as they planned, they all met again in Tiffany's beach house to celebrate Archy and Francine's first anniversary on Provincetown Bay, and he might even have a partner then.

"What are you, a pilgrim?"

"Sort of Pop, sort of."

Count No Man Unhappy . . .
(a short story with a chorus)

Until he is dead, do not yet call a man happy, but only lucky.
(Herodotus attributed these words to Solon, 638- 590 B.C.)

"*Until I kick the bucket, I'll still play Vegas!*"
(Milton Berle, 1908-2002)

"*Go ahead, become a millionaire, see if I care.*"
(Abraham Ben Jacob)

1

Ludwig Fried, ruminator, connoisseur of ambivalence, deep into retirement, still writing, still longing for a breakthrough with a major publication, *The New Yorker*, *Atlantic*, looked back on his life through his introspective rear-view mirror as he sat in his provincial garden in Western New York on a brightly moonlit midsummer evening.

"Easier for a *Lucky Strike* to get through the eye of a needle," he thought he heard his late father say.

Camel, Pop, camel.

"Camel, *schlemiel*, big deal, it's all the same, but keep it up, your pecker, too, don't waffle so much. You're not the chef at Lindy's."

You're living in the past.

"So where else could I be, wise guy?"

Ludwig leaned back in his hunter green Adirondack chair, an unexpected letter of invitation from Yangon University Myanmar in one hand, a glass of scotch in the other. A new Department of American Studies wanted him to discuss his "Exilic Literature *after* the Holocaust," his one article that had made a ripple in the academic pond early in his career. It made him somewhat anxious now to think that the article, though it had made a splash long ago, might upset the military censors.

Ludwig assumed they were planted in universities, even if Aung San Suu Kyi was State Counselor, virtually President. If his talk came to the attention of the still powerful military junta, they might think he was referring somehow to the brutal oppression of the Moslem minority, the Rohingyas, in the western province on the shores of the Bay of Bengal.

"I see you've been doing your homework. I didn't pay for you to go to Harvard for nothing."

Columbia, Pop, Columbia.

"Whatever. Ivy grows on old *goyisher* walls."

Having grown up in the shadow of the Holocaust, it didn't take much for Ludwig to imagine that there was always some version of the Gestapo ready to knock on your door and take you away never to return again. Myanmar would be no exception.

It wasn't much of a risk, but Ludwig the academic could imagine danger lurking around the bend of a creek. He sometimes dreamed that he might live a life and write a story like Graham Greene, but when he woke up, he understood what Freud meant by *wish-fulfillment*.

He would have preferred old "Rangoon" and "Burma" instead of Myanmar, echoes of high school assemblies, Oley Speaks 1907 musical version of Kipling's "Mandalay." The world had changed, but he was still, too often, clunkin' on the Irrawaddy of the past.

It might be that no time was left to "smite the sounding furrows," and there was now a large group of Burmese immigrants in Buffalo, some even in the suburbs.

He might be able to help them somehow when he returned, if he left.

He had retreated in many ways to his evergreen circled garden, a kind of bower, but no paradise, no Eve in sight, and took some comfort in the lingering twilight of the summer solstice on the right bank of Ellicott Creek, an obscure stream that gurgled past his house on Garrison Road in Amherst, New York, an affluent suburb of Buffalo. Not Scarsdale, but still affluent. He was, in some ways, like the stream.

Only recently had he been curious enough to find out, thanks to MapQuest, the origin and terminus of the stream.

Starting behind City Hall in the Village of Williamsville, founded in 1818, it flowed to Aero Drive, an unpaved road that ran under the end of a runway at the Buffalo Niagara International Airport.

"You call that international? It's no JFK by me, but still it's an airport. Don't forget your camp song, 'Up in the air junior birdman. . . .' Keep flapping your wings, Kid."

I hear you, Pop, I remember what Mother said, "I raised you to fly the coop."

The stream ended at the edge of a small cemetery from the War of 1812, recently unearthed. For some reason, this information interested him now, even seemed important.

It was his favorite time of year, however briefly it lasted, the lengthening of light before the onset of its incremental narrowing, an Elizabethan paradox. Even if he hadn't felt favored by the gods of Mt. Olympus, the Eight Immortals of China, or their modern equivalents—a hustling literary agent and an invitation to appear on "Charlie Rose" to discuss his "latest"—there still, improbably, might be time to "make it."

This was, after all, the ambition of all American writers he had known, in a sports-crazy country where wining Big Time was the only thing that mattered, a country of gladiators with college degrees: Boise State, Stanford, "Bama." Long gone, even as memory, were the days of the Festival of Dionysus when Sophocles' tragedies duked it out with those of Aeschylus.

Ludwig was tired of being a *minor print writer* in the digital age where too many online editors had given him the finger. Not delusional, he was pretty sure, he couldn't claim the stature of Matthew Arnold, T.S. Eliot, or Lionel Trilling, but the word "online" stuck in his literary throat like a fishbone that would fillet his sensibility. A grandchild of immigrants and street peddlers, driven to make a place for themselves in America, he still hoped against hope to win a National Book Award.

"That's my boy, a real dreamer."

Even though he was in the far-turn of his life . . .

"You've got that right, sonny boy," he heard his late garment-center-salesman father say in his nasal Mott Street accent. "It ain't Belmont, but life is a horse race and you're a jockey. Use the whip, for Crissakes. Run for the roses before they wilt."

. . . and even though he sometimes thought he heard the wind chimes at midnight and the suction of the grim reaper's vacuum cleaner in the dead of a Buffalo winter, the frigid zone where academic tenure at a state university, a writer's retreat, a brick (if not ivory) tower, had set him down, he still wondered if the summer solstice didn't hold a message for him: *you still have some time, it's still light out*.

"Here, Luddy, borrow my BULOVA, the hands don't move, I bought it from Al Singer, the 'Bronx Beauty,' you remember him, he used to come to the showroom when he needed a sawbuck."

Of course I remember Al. Poor guy, never recovered from the loss to Tony Canzoneri in 1930, retina detached, Madison Square Garden. And I know you're my cut-man, Pop, I know you're in my corner, but relax, I've got to work this through myself. I'm in the ring, not you.

"I'll try, but I worry."

That's the problem, your worry makes me worry.

"Okay, I'll go to the Stage Deli for a while."

Good idea. Have a tongue sandwich for me, but keep quiet for a change.

"Who are you, the Delilama?"

Wise guy.

Maybe he had stepped out of the ring and the Big Top too soon and protected himself by acting as if he was a semi-loser who lived in the shadows of the heavy hitters.

"Maybe they weren't such heavy hitters. Ask them. Find out."

They're gone, Pop, they're gone.

"Maybe not. Am I?"

I hear you, I hear you.

Ludwig had built a comfortable world in which to come to terms with what his late mother called "end of life issues."

It even included a small gazebo in the shape of a Ming Dynasty Tea House so that he could sit out in the rain, even in a light snow, and recall the years he had spent as a lecturer in Hong Kong and Asia, the splash of neon light in Victoria harbor, the glitter of Central District as the Star Ferry approached the dock, affluent ex-pats sipping G.H. Mumm champagne on the upper deck.

On those few winter nights when he could sit in the gazebo, a brazier of hot coals near his feet, sniffing a tumbler of cognac, he thought of himself sometimes as living in a Currier and Ives print or a Hokusai woodcut. Motionless, he thought of the cabin of the barge captain, Jean, in Vigo's *L'Atalante*, surrounded by *objets* of past sea-voyages. He thought also of his own "memorabilia highway," as he called it, a shelf of souvenirs from his past world travels: ostrich shell, South Africa; shofar, Israel; brass skewers, Turkey; pewter kris, Malaysia; porcelain Buddha, Hong Kong; celadon vase, Korea. Not a winner, perhaps, but he wasn't a loser, global-wise.

It was clear now, on this summer solstice evening, perhaps because it was the twilight of his life, that he was paddling his introspective canoe slowly towards Freud's version of the Styx—Thanatos. His real Adirondack canoe had been tied up, unused, for some time at the small dock where his lawn edged the creek.

He had enjoyed a few splashes of success in the literary creeks of Western New York—a story in a small magazine in Oklahoma or Ohio, the odd lecture on "Alienation, Impotence, and Loss in American Literature" at Hobart, St. Bonaventure, Keuka Junior College, and some other minor institutions around the Finger Lakes, but not the Big Finger, Cornell.

He had left behind, perhaps prematurely, the grand Hemingwayesque ambitions he had floated on the current of the majestic Hudson River of his adolescent years. He had outlived Hem, poor guy, but Hem's work had outlived Hem.

"You hit the nail on the balls. . . ."

Head.

"Okay, Head, smead, what's the diff? You listened to that pipsqueak, Shorty Epstein, the one who said that you both were professors in the Grapefruit League. You listened to him, *shmuck.*"

You remember Shorty? That was so long ago. He's gone. You may run into him. Give him the finger for me, just kidding, He gave it to himself.

Ludwig suddenly could see the long span of his life. How much longer could it be? He had come to Buffalo in 1967; now it was 2017. Of course, there was no time or death in the Macy's basement of the unconscious, so it didn't feel that long in retrospect. Like an old movie he had seen in his young manhood—*Roshoman*, *Twelve Angry Men*, *Some Like It Hot*, *Ninoctchka*, *Body and Soul.* They never seem dated.

But move it back a few centuries, he thought, a game he sometimes played: 1867-1917; 1767-1817; 1667-1717.

1567-1617. From the end of the Civil War to America's entry into WWI; pre-Revolutionary American to the end of the War of 1812—the Battle of Lake Erie; the founding of Harvard to the Hartford Wits; three years after the birth of Shakespeare to a year after his death.

Not easy to imagine these great arcs of time having anything to do with his life, but they did, and when this truth hit him like a bolt from the blue, he almost fell out of his Adirondack chair.

"Bolts?"

Bolt, Pop, bolt.

He now snapped out of his ruminative semi-coma. Rumination . . . a room with ruminations, he had lived in one too long, it now seemed clear, but how to get out of it?

"Remember, kid, I told you to stay out of rooms when you occupied the President's Office in 1970 and got arrested."

One of your great suggestions.

But did it make sense to accept the invitation to lecture in Myanmar, a program that an old flame in the Foreign Service, posted in old Rangoon, now Yangon, must have managed to wrangle for him? Did it make sense for him to fly halfway around the world, economy class, and end up semi-lame, his sciatica climbing from his big right toe to his hip, to share some warning signals about survival with a small audience who might or might not understand English? Well, if nothing else, there always was the possibility of meeting 'a Burma girl a-settin'.'

"That's my boy, still a dreamer. So what are you, a man or a *pisher*? Get off your rump, my *kaddish*. I hear the Electrolux humming, and it don't sound like old blue eyes."

Don't worry, Pop, I'm no Oblomov.

"Oblomov, did I know him? A buyer for J.C. Penny? Sounds familiar."

Forget it, Pop. Your grandfather might have met him, not you. He never got off his ass.

"So you know what I mean, good."

Didn't it make more sense to stay in his garden, sit in the gazebo during a light summer rain, and accept the fact that he had accomplished all that he was likely to achieve? After all, he wasn't a big shot like the big bulbs who had lit up the department in the early days.

There seemed to be a star in every other office when he arrived at The State University of Western New York, a real planetarium of illuminated Fabergé eggheads. It had made him feel like a firefly, emitting imperceptible pulses of light in the dimly lit Quonset huts where they taught.

He knew that some of them were burnt-out stars, intellectually disabled, like feisty Lionel Abel (R.I.P., sort of), intellectual assassin, Stalinist anti-Stalinist. Still, but not self-assured, Ludwig had felt that he was living in their shadows—darkness at morning, noon, and twilight, a mini-Arthur Koestler.

"I didn't come from so far to hear this crap, Luddy. Remember where we came from, we move uptown, kid, we don't stop at 14th Street, M. Klein's Basement."

Nothing really held him back now. Long divorced, his daughter and family lived in Israel. His last lady friend, an Assistant Professor of Archeology, had left him to work on a dig in Anatolia, a wall in a hole.

"But *I'm* an old site," he had quipped, helplessly.

"Not as interesting as a real ruin, Ephesus, sorry, Lud, nothing personal. You're a great old guy, but not a shard. I need to earn tenure."

He understood and retreated then, a year ago, to his gazebo where he nursed a double scotch, *Chivas Regal*, and stared at the illuminated globe that hung from its crimson cedar rafter, a reminder of the parts of the world he had managed somehow to see.

Well, he had until July 4th to make up his mind, a "fortnight," as the suave Brit., J. Lockwood Windsor, might have said. A graduate of the Dragon School, King's College, Cambridge, and Princeton, "Wind" had been Ludwig's office mate for a year before he had been made a Fellow of All Souls College, Oxford. His definitive deconstructive biography, of Samuel Pepys, *Epistolary Epistemology*, had made him a hot commodity in 17th century studies.

Yes, he had a fortnight or "Two fucking weeks," as Lester "Beaver King" Finebloom, yang to Windsor's yin, might have said. Raised in Newark, nose tackle at Rutgers, Rhodes Scholar, Harvard Junior Fellow, Hell's Angels

(Hon.), Finebloom was the author, second book, of a best-selling biography, *Kick Ass: Kerouac's Embodied Cosmos.*

Once, sitting next to Ludwig at a department meeting, listening to Windsor hold forth in admiralty English, "Les" had whispered in his ear, "Bullshit, Lud, good thing he's leaving. He'd rather kiss at High Table than ride a Harley Davidson like me, ass to the wind. He may be leaving, but he isn't going anywhere."

Going to Myanmar might not mean anything to Windsor or Beaver King. No Oxford don or souped-up Finebloom, the trip might not augment his reputation and win him a Guggenheim. No academic rough rider, a groupie in every Starbucks, he had to admit that he still felt the pull of the East, "somewhere East of Suez."

Now he seemed to see a shadow standing under the arch of the teahouse, an All Soul's scarf neatly draped over his pinstriped Saville Row suit, eyes sunken in Whistler-like grey shadows, Lionel Trilling in a dark mood.

"You've got it wrong, Ludwig, old boy, terribly wrong. I had nothing to say after my plash in the academic pool. The old pedantic well went dry, no gas left in the antiquarian tank."

It can't be, Wind, everything about you was bespoke. You made me feel as if I shopped at Goodwill.

"Style isn't the man, old chap, I can tell you that. Take away this scarf and suit, and you'll see a man, a recovering alcoholic, who slaves over entries for the *Encyclopedia of British Diaries* at three in the morning to salvage some pride, a hollow man, a thinking reed become a straw."

Not you, Wind.

"No wind in the sails, Lud, believe me. Keep sailing, listen to those 'temple-bells.'"

It must be the Chivas, Ludwig thought, taking another shot.

"Maybe not, asshole, maybe not," Les blurted in Ludwig's inner ear.

I'll be fucked.

"You wish. Let me go with you, buddy, and I'll try to show you how to snag some Burmese beaver."

A silhouette of Finebloom—Stetson lowered over his bushy eyebrows, hair tonsured like the rim of a volcano, silver-studded Harley jacket turned up at the collar, seemed to be standing next to Lockwood, shoulders slumped, beer-belly sagging—seemed to be cupping its crotch protectively.

Me, a buddy? No chance, Les. I'm not a big prick like you, and since when do you 'try'? You step over people, trample, go right to the top. That's why you're Beaver King.

"I said, 'try to show you,' *putz*, you never understood."

What?

The silhouette's shoulders drooped lower. He spoke haltingly. "I'm not well. . . . I don't have much time left . . . maybe six months, no friends, even 'Beaver Queen' ditched me when she found out how many pelts I had stroked."

I'll be damned. You could knock me over with a feather.

"I always felt like a feather, Lud, I knew I was no Norman Mailer, no Harold Bloom, but I needed you all to think I was, it's all clear now, I was fighting for my life, recognition, respect. Can you understand? I apologize."

But you weren't a lightweight, you had that first book that defined a new field—THE ASSHOLE IS A GRAVE: THE CASE FOR PRISON REFORM. You were our ithyphallus.

"But I wanted more, Lud, MORE should be my epitaph."

The shadowy figure leaned forward and whispered, almost stuttered. "I have a confession, Lud . . . I always thought . . . I had . . . a little one . . . I wanted a larger . . ." The shadow clutched his crotch more tightly. ". . . A bigger career, I got them mixed up, I was farblongjet, a little like you. Now I can tell you, maybe it will help both of us."

You even know some Yiddish?

"Didn't want anyone to know I was from Newark."

Windsor chimed in. "What kind of 'jet'? Sounds as if we're in the same sinking boat, Lester, but I thought you were our anchor, dear boy, in the old days, ballast in the hold to keep us from drifting too far from real life. Don't tell me you had a hole in the bottom of the bucket, too. You, a *little one*? Hard to believe."

"*Hard* was my problem, Wind, I never should have called you a Pepys-squeak. I was, I was an asshole to say it."

"Your field at the time, old sport, I understood, no problem."

If what he had heard, or thought he had heard, was true, not just a somewhat tipsy auditory delusion, or, if that, true nonetheless, a deep intuition and important, a belief that the words were true, that would make all the difference.

Ruminations, daydreams, hallucinations, nightmares—it didn't matter where the truth came from, so long as it came in time to change one's life, especially if the life was your own.

"Listen to yourself, Luddy. Show 'em what you're made of."

I'll be damned, maybe it wasn't too late.

2

Ready or not, Ludwig realized, the time had come to act, to test the story he had made up about himself. Maybe he had let his literary frustrations, envy, muted resentments, and exile from Manhattan's literary circles shrink his grand ambitions and choke the windpipe of his self-esteem. Unable to face his buried resentments, he had retreated to the shadows of his garden. He had put Les and Wind on plinths and sat on a stool.

"What, live like a turtle, like me?"

If he could have been so wrong about Les and Wind, why couldn't he have been equally off base about himself? After all, you didn't have to go on a safari to hunt for truths about the human experience.

"Good question, Luddy. And you're not playing softball in the schoolyard anymore."

He wasn't Hamlet and he wasn't up the creek without a paddle. In fact, his canoe was neatly secured against the side of his dock. If he was going to paddle up the Irrawaddy and hear the tinkle of the temple bells, he needed to practice feathering his oars.

Although it was near midnight, there were enough house lights casting a glow across the creek for him to paddle safely towards a spot where he could see some jets coming in over the glide-path, a reminder, if he needed one, that people were on the move.

As he stood up, a little wobbly from having been stuck in his chair so long, he heard the light toll of his neighbor's wind chimes. Encouraged by the soothing sounds, he ambled to the dock.

Centering himself on the seat, Ludwig untied the canoe and began to paddle towards what looked like a string of illuminated Chinese lanterns a quarter of a mile in the distance. He wasn't sure if he was paddling upstream or downstream or if the creek had a stream, but it didn't matter—he was paddling, not drifting.

"Better to stroke than have one. Think of me."

I say Kaddish, Pop.

As the canoe cut through the water, creating a V-shaped ripple, Ludwig thought of Shorty Epstein, coxswain for the 1960 Columbia crew, and wondered what the little naysayer-of-old would think of his midsummer evening voyage.

"Give it up, Lud, you're too old to set sail. Who do you think you are, Odysseus? I told you years ago, we're landlubbers, we're from the Bronx, we didn't go to Annapolis. Turn around. Shoulder your oars."

Suddenly, imagining Shorty leading a chorus of naysayers in a moss-covered amphitheater, Ludwig laughed, paddled faster, and pressed on.

"Better than pressing a pair of pants in a sweatshop. I didn't send you to Yale for nothing."

Columbia, Pop, Columbia.

"Gem of the Ocean?"

116th Street and Broadway, remember?

"It's not Alzheimer's, Luddy, it was just so long ago."

His oar seemed to be gliding more easily through the water.

"You'd do better with Kierkegaard's *Either Or!*" Shorty called out in Ludwig's inner Coliseum.

As the canoe approached the bend in the creek where the reflection of the moonlight in the water merged with the glow of the lanterns, he thought he heard muted weeping. It was, unmistakably, a woman's.

He gently stopped the forward movement of the canoe to take a closer look without disturbing her. She sat, a shawl over her shoulders, legs crossed in a prayerful position, her hands interwoven over her face like the filigreed eaves of a Thai temple.

"No one can find them," she seemed to be saying. She then unlocked her hands, uplifted her face, and extended her arms towards the creek, maybe towards him, he wasn't sure. "I can't reach them, help, someone help them, please help." She then lowered her head, covered her face, and seemed to be praying again.

He thought about saying something to her, but then thought better about it. She needed help, but she needed to be alone now. He understood that deeply. He had been, too long, a connoisseur of aloneness and sorrow.

"You've been pampering yourself, Lefty, hit the line," his old football coach screamed in his inner gridiron. He thought of Gatsby reaching for the green light. Her posture reminded him of something more tragic, but what was it? And then an image of Picasso's *Rape of the Sabine Women* bubbled up to the surface of his mind and behind it—like a following ripple, out of the deep past, the brain's Fort Knox vault—a moment in the *Aeneid*. . . .

"Give me a break, Lud," Les sneered, "no one remembers that ancient crap."

"I do, old sport," Wind chimed in. "when Aeneas, entering a temple in Carthage, sees a mural of the Trojan War in which so many of his comrades had died, cries and says, "There are tears for events and mortal things touch the soul."

"At least you spared us Latin, asshole."

"What do you know, Finebloom?" his father echoed, "he's a Columbia man."

Thanks Pop.

Then the Latin spouted up from the fountain of memory . . . *sunt lachrimae rerum et mentum mortalia tangent*. . . .

He thought of Hemingway: "The world breaks everyone and afterward some are strong at the broken places." Maybe Ludwig had stepped out of the ring too soon. It was at least clear that he had been wrong about many things, including the measure he had taken of himself.

"Al would have fought again, if he could've, Luddy."

"You've still got a jab, kid, you still can throw a punch."

"At you too?"

"Never left you."

Head lowered, he stroked more vigorously now. He didn't want the weeping woman to see him staring at her.

After a few minutes, hearing the roar of engines, he back-paddled, looked up, and realized he was at the end of the stream in a hollow below the end of the runway.

Looking up, he could see the logo of the 737 in the flashing taillight: UNITED. Heart pumping like the turbines at Niagara Falls Power Station, he felt as if he might be on the verge of a mission. For all he knew, the weeping woman might be Burmese or Syrian, even Sudanese. There were many immigrants and refugees in Buffalo. New York City didn't get all of those who had lost or fled their homelands.

He still had some time to make up his mind about accepting the invitation to Burma, but it would be a hard trip for someone like Ludwig. He was, after all, old, alone, sciatica moving up and down his right leg like the loose carriage of a Remington typewriter.

A ruminator in a world that called for action, a writer in an age of sound bites, his work was, as one friend had written to him, "quietly moving," another, "a call of the mild." One thing was clear—he couldn't change if he didn't raise his voice and take some risks.

"We're betting on you," the chorus of yea-sayers said in unison.

Engines powered up, the plane roared down the runway and up into the night air. He hoped the skies would be friendly for these night passengers, and the censors on vacation if he decided to make the trip, and told the students what human rights he thought they really should be fighting for.

Many years ago on a lecture tour of China, he had promised the Political Affairs Officer at the US Embassy on Beijing that he wouldn't mention the *Laogai*, China's Gulag. He wouldn't make any promises this time, except to himself.

I may have gotten lucky, he thought, and started paddling home. Although he was panting, everything seemed to be flowing.

One Day at the End of His World

Each of us when separated . . . is but . . . half of a man, and he is always looking for the other half.

Aristophanes' Speech (Plato's *Symposium)*

Ludwig Fried, no Lindberg, John Glenn, nor Richard Branson, forget Vasco Da Gama, looked a little manically for the right button in his Boeing Dreamliner 767 Emirates Air luxury panel-enclosed seat, more like a La-Z-Boy recliner, so he could lie matzo-flat and get some shuteye as the plane hummed, almost whispered, quietly at thirty-eight thousand feet over the Persian Gulf en route from Lisbon to Dubai and then Yangon, in early March.

"What the hell are you doing up here? And business class, no less, fancy-schmancy, a real big shot, all of a sudden he thinks he's Marco Polo. You're better off in Boca this time of year."

But you told me to get off my butt, Pop, remember? 'Up in the air junior birdman . . . keep flapping your wings keep looking for the big plot.'

"Forget plots, I know too much about them, and I didn't say so far, the Arab world, for crissakes."

Buddhist, Pop, old Burma.

"Did they convert in Dubai?"

En route.

"In French or Yiddish, no matter how long, you're stopping with the Moslems. In a second you could be disappeared."

Go to sleep, give me break.

"You should be so lucky, you always said we didn't talk enough."

That was then, this is now.

"Now, then, what's the dif, I'm still your father."

Okay, but remember what you said, "Get off your ass, show 'em what you're made of."

"I didn't say the armpit of Africa."

It's Asia.

"Still an armpit."

Ludwig's late father, Izzy Fried, a son of Mott Street, couldn't sleep either, it seemed, but, then, there was neither night nor day in Freud's basement, Ludwig's underground world, the mind's subway, whatever it was.

Unable to sleep, no Rip Van Winkle, he hit a few of the icons on the TV screen and was able, small miracle for him, klutz to the lack of manner born, to call up the "Flight Route" map with a photo-inset that allowed him to see the terrain over which he was flying on this cloudless and starry night.

"My son the astronaut, what are you, a night-mail pilot, Saint-Exupéry?"

Just two weeks of lectures in Yangon, Pop.

"So what's wrong with your university?"

Retired, two years ago.

"But why so far? And don't forget ISIS. Who knows who's out there?"

Yes, why so far? Especially for someone who was a nervous flyer. For years Ludwig had thought that he might blow off an engine if he flushed the toilet in flight, to say nothing of staying up all night listening to the engines to keep them whirring.

"What? Rolls Royce has feelings?"

But he had gotten over those anxieties after giving many lectures "On Aloneness and Anonymity in American Literature" in many countries, his one essay that had become a "citation classic," his platform for overseas travel. Readers of small magazines and professors loved alienation.

His ambitions had overcome those specific symptoms, if not a general sense of dread about losing himself or getting lost, his "identity theme," as some Madison Avenue doctor of the mind had called it. But he managed to sit half-upright and look at the graphic trajectory of the route as well as photo-images of the earth below as the Dreamliner started its descent towards Dubai.

"Better you should be a *schmatte* salesman than make this crazy trip to nowhere."

It's not nowhere, Pop, it's Yangon.

"Stay home, watch a Crosby and Hope movie—*Miami Beach*.

But his father had a point. The old street savvy garment center salesman, who had pounded the pavement on W. 37th Street for half a century, knew his customers.

"You're right, sonny boy, you can't bullshit a bullshitter. Don't get me wrong, I had dreams too, ship out on a German freighter, see the world, leave the sweatshops behind, but I got cold feet, heard my mother crying. Better not to have dreams. Every time I see a cruise ship pull out of Port Everglades, Trinidad bound, I think about what I missed, better to burn the phony dreams."

You can see from up there?

"Not sure up, but wide-angle vision, like a drone."

His father might be right: better not to have dreams. But he felt incomplete, just another writer in a small college on the edge of the Great Lakes. Not a unique fate, but his, and his clock was ticking, not quiet, digital, the Big Ben of the unlived life, the great American theme, but his. If he was going to snag the brass ring, he had to get on the carousel.

"Major, minor, another, what's the dif, boychik? Up here everyone's uncreated equal, a mote under the aspect of eternity and infinity. Who could be a big shot when you know you're a *nebbish* in a nebula."

Are you sure you're you? Have you been going to night school?

"Plenty of time on my hands and who else would care so much?"

But he still was looking for the big story, the one that would put him on the map, the knockout punch: an agent, book deal, major review in *The New York Times*. He hadn't "folded his wigwam" yet, as his mother used to say.

"Think small, Luddy, look at me. I tried *big,* factory in Cuba, look what happened! Better a store for intimate apparel in Great Neck. My brother, Hesh, was right, 'Think small, Izzy. Better bikinis than Bikini Atoll!'"

You should have tried stand-up comedy, Pop.

"Wish I could sit-down, no chairs here like *Our Town.*"

You've learned so much, how did it happen?

"I've been auditing your dreams."

The darkness below, except for the dim lights from some scattered villages or nomadic encampments, now gave way to a tracery of lights that separated the landmass from the Arabian Gulf. Narrow bracelets of light soon formed diamond and pendant shaped patterns. He didn't know if these patterns were the outlines of the airfield or advertisements for Dubai's fabled wealth, but, then, the glittering arc of the Dubai Marina came into view.

It was the real, if *sur*real, deal. F. Scott Fitzgerald would have been jealous and Van Gogh might have cut off his other ear. As Ludwig scanned the arc of lights in the distance, he had a momentary impulse to cancel the trip to Yangon and spend a few days in Dubai, the Hong Kong of the Middle East, Disney World in sheik's clothing, but then he remembered his bank account, *dim sum*, not the edible, and came to his senses.

* * *

Sitting in the business class lounge of Dubai's International Terminal, an hour to wait before he boarded the next flight for Yangon, Ludwig looked at the gleaming high rises and hotels that he could see in the distance through the gold-edged floor-to-ceiling windows, the *new* New World.

The sail-shaped Burj Al Arab at 1000 feet rose above the other glitzy hotels and leaned towards the Gulf like Kareem's skyhook. The Fairmont Palm and Palm Jumeirah were dim bulbs against the radiance of the Brancusi-like Five Star tribute to the oil-rich Gulf state.

He thought of Frank Lloyd Wright's sketch of a mile-high skyscraper that would overlook all of Chicago and Lake Michigan, but it was only a drawing. The Empire State Building alone, as seen in 1931, might have held a candle to this colossus of luxury as an object of wonder, this glittering tribute to man's capacity for self-indulgence.

"Good to see you got a word in for Manhattan, you're a real Harvard snob."

Columbia, Pop, like Obama. Time you went to sleep."

"Distance" was a key word for him, he now understood, if it hadn't been clear before. He had been reaching out for decades and failing to grasp life's, at least Fifth Avenue's, trophies: literary success and an artsy, lithe, intelligent, and passionate, even loyal, Sarah Lawrence graduate on his arm.

"The Grand Concourse and City College would have made more sense. Burn the phony dream, Luddy. I know, here's a Zippo lighter."

The 7th Avenue *schlepper* might have a point, but the Old Man's early success, before the IRS busted him, had made the phony dreams, if that's what they were, possible. He had inherited the dream in his Bronx childhood, Grand Course, but still the Bronx, not Manhattan, and he felt some responsibility for making it come true, phony or not.

He thought of Goya's *The Sleep of Reason Produces Monsters*. It was something like the obverse of his reverse: *The Day-Dream of the Lower East Side Produces Ambition*.

"What do the *goyim* have to do with it?"

Goya, Pop, Goya!

"You need some sleep, give it a rest. Next thing you know, I'll be thinking about how the IRS broke me so I couldn't pay for your third year at Yale . . ."

Columbia.

". . . and sent you to Europe so you could chauffeur your crazy Uncle Hesh around."

But I met Hemingway.

"Big deal, look what happened to him."

His father had a point: he was wasting his time with too many ifs.

"Better you should be happy."

Just as Ludwig was about to nod off, head sinking into a plush silk cushion, with *Fly First Class* embroidered on it, he heard the announcement to board the flight for Yangon.

"Bon voyage, sonny boy, have some egg foo yung for me.

Burma, Pop, not the House of Chan.

"Better Broadway, but, whatever, I've got your back. You don't have to prove anything to me, only to yourself."

Is this you talking?

"I let you down when I went broke, I had to find ways to make up for it."

As Ludwig headed towards the stairway to the plane, he glanced at the kaleidoscope of lights beyond the airport and wondered if he wasn't going too far, if it made sense to jump ship now. He hesitated at the first step, looked around, and knew that he had to find out if he was chasing an illusion.

"You may be a *schmuck*, Luddy, but no son of mine takes a dive."

Slightly nauseated, he hesitated, but knew he couldn't turn back. It wasn't the point of no return, but it felt as if he were walking the plank.

"You're no Irwin Shaw, kid, but, hey, give it a shot, I may have jumped ship too soon."

Up there you have a lending library?

"Easy, Ludwig, you're beginning to sound like me. Remember, you're a Yale man."

Columbia, 116th Street, Manhattan, Pop, Uptown, but Manhattan.

* * *

Ludwig had been informed at the last minute that he would arrive on the eve of a water festival in honor of Aung San Suu Kyi's 1991 Nobel Peace Prize, an unexpected move by the former military junta to make their influence clear. So he was disappointed, but not surprised that he found the Yangon airport virtually empty as he approached the visa window, not sure if his letter of invitation, certifying that he was a "foreign expert," would satisfy the Talmudic scrutiny of the sullen officer in a crumpled military uniform.

Once in Shengdu he had, American-style, told the Chair of the Literary Cadre that he was *half an expert*, and he had been told that the university would complain to the US Embassy. He wouldn't kid around this time.

The official pored over the documents, gave Ludwig the once over, and then asked, "True expert?"

Tempted to say, "half," his position in life, it seemed, Ludwig nodded.

"One hundred dollars for visa."

"Credit card, okay?" he asked.

"Only uncrushed dollars."

His travel agent had told him about this seemingly bizarre demand for crisp, unwrinkled currency, and he had come with a small stash of them and passed one under the Plexiglas barrier.

The officer held up against a screen, snapped it a few times, and then stamped Ludwig's passport. "Good money, welcome to Myanmar, we're a poor country, we need foreign experts."

"Watch out you don't get crushed, Luddy."

I know about being crushed, Pop, don't worry.

"You're telling me, I'm an expert."

Only a few people milled around the Baggage Claim area, so it was easy for Ludwig to find his L.L. Bean backpack. For the first time in his life, despite apprehensions, he had decided to act like an adventurer, a belated trekker on a Lonely Planet trail. Maybe not act, but act like.

"A real Hillary, all you need is a Tenzing."

You've got Google, too?

Years ago, a high class phony had told Ludwig, "Pretend you're the person you want to be. Who knows? You might become him." It had worked for Les Finebloom, erstwhile colleague, *chevalier* of a lower order, faux multiculturalist, now Chair of Global Ethnicity Studies at Hobart, bank account in Geneva—Switzerland, not New York. It might work for him—Ludwig Fried's *Burmese Nights*, homage to Orwell.

"Get a hold of yourself, be yourself, even if it makes me nervous."

Ludwig looked eagerly and anxiously through the glass partition that separated the Baggage Claim area from the arrival terminal. Among the few people who stood behind the barrier, only one, a frail young man in a faded blue *loongi*, held a placard: "Welcome to Dr. Fried!"

Well, he was technically a doctor, but not someone who could help you if you had a hernia. Real writers, at least the ones he admired, hadn't gone to graduate school. Some good ones had, but they hadn't been the ones who tattooed his psyche in his adolescence.

He waved at the young man, who looked as if he could use a good meal, pointed at himself, and smiled. He flexed his fingers a few times to indicate that he would be out in a few minutes.

When he cleared Customs, "nothing to declare," and walked into the waiting area, he was struck by the oppressive heat and humidity.

"Welcome to Myanmar," the young man said. "My name is Thet Ko Ko, you can call me Ko Ko. The director sends his apologies. Because of the sudden holiday, no one else was free to come. He and the staff will meet you on Monday. I'll take you to your hotel. Ko Ko will be your friendly guide until then."

"What day is it now?" Ludwig asked.

"Friday."

He knew it would be a long weekend, maybe too long, but it was too early to tell what his two weeks in another country would turn out to be like.

"You wait, sir, I'll get the VW and then drive you to your nice hotel, just across from the college."

Ludwig had googled the hotel: *Lotus Boutique* and been pleased to see photos of an illuminated koi pond, a rooftop terrace that faced a gold-domed pagoda, and some lacquered objects, a tapestry of elephants hauling teak out of a steep ravine. Thinking of the map that had drawn him to Hong Kong some years before—splashes of neon color and reflections of glitzy high rises in Victoria Harbor—he wondered if the *Lotus Boutique* would be consonant with the images that had inspired him to make the trip. He didn't have to be a magician or French literary critic to think that the image and the reality might be different. . . .

"Don't tell me you take those frogs seriously, Luddy."

Since when are you into French literary theory? You didn't even finish high school. And don't you ever sleep?

"Night school, Luddy, long nights, and I don't sleep when you're thinking or dreaming. I'm your father, remember Anchises?

Next thing I know, you'll tell me I'm Aeneas.

"You left home, didn't you, looking for a new one? I told you to stay put, putz around in your own garden like

Voltaire, but you hit the road, a real Kerouac, and I had to stay with you, I'm your father. You want to be a big-shot, to stand out, I said you could end up in a bamboo cage for saying the wrong thing, I can see the headline: *Ludwig Fried Detained as Mossad Agent.*"

But the *Lotus Boutique* even might be better, he thought: a hammock covered with a mosquito net that swayed under a banyan tree. He once had stayed in a hotel like that in Kerala near the beach where Vasco da Gama had landed. That was the trip he had hoped would be a bestseller: Site-Seeing in the Diaspora.

That was the trip when he had traveled for a week with the aspiring Bombay actress, Manju, daughter of a diamond merchant, who had sung *Summertime* for him one night on the beach, her gold embossed sari glittering in the moonlight.

"And you call yourself a loser?"

The book was turned down, too colonial, the editor said.

"And the girl?"

She became a nurse when she saw what life was like outside of Bombay's gold coast. She wrote to me later and said that stars belonged in heaven.

"I see some of them, but I'd rather have Hindu nookie."

Grow up, Pop.

"Does anyone?"

* * *

The VW squeezed through an alley and pulled up in front of the *Lotus Boutique,* a three storey building that stood at end of a small square. A chipped fountain in the middle of the square bubbled brackish water over a small Buddha. Ko Ko opened the car-door for him.

"Here you are, sir, your home away from home." He smiled with the pleasure of someone who knew American idioms from TV shows.

"Is the school far away?"

"There, sir." He pointed. "Just across from your new home."

Ludwig looked up. A tin sign hung from the moss-covered third floor balcony of a commercial building: *Welcome to Parami Prep!* "What does 'Parami' mean?"

"An old Sanskrit word—virtue, learning through dialogue."

"You should be lecturing, Ko Ko. Not me."

"Too late for me, sir, I'm lucky to be a chauffeur at this new school in a new Myanmar. Many people have to beg in front of the hotels to stay alive. Without this job, I'm nobody again, invisible, alone, unknown."

A group of begging women, faces daubed with what looked like war paint, sat cross-legged around the fountain. As Ludwig looked at them, each made a gesture of touching her right forearm with her left hand, and extended a bowl of mysterious looking nuts. Ludwig looked questioningly at Ko Ko.

"A sign of respect, sir."

One of the women, voluptuous, with eyes like transparent jade, looked imploringly at him, gestured towards the *Lotus Boutique,* and let him see that she was bare-breasted under her shawl. He didn't know if it was poverty or solicitation, but he wondered if he would reach to her later in the evening to help him get through a long night in a windowless room.

"And the makeup?"

"*Thanakha*, a traditional way in which village women protect against the heat and preserve their beauty. Much wisdom has come from the tribal people."

"Even the Rohingyas?"

"Better to not talk about them, sir."

Button your lip, Luddy, play it safe.

"Here, let me carry your backpack. Time to see your new home."

Ludwig's "home" turned out to be a neat, but sweltering and windowless room. Years ago he had heard a lecture on "Descartes' Dream" about the night in which the philosopher had conceived of the "cogito" in an "oppressively hot room" near Munich. Ludwig found the room so hot that it seemed clear to him that he would be likely to think: *I shrink, therefore I was.*

"I got out of the tenement, Luddy, you're not trapped."

A cracked wooden fan creaked slowly on a high ceiling.

'Teak, sir, our national wood. My father used an elephant to drag the trees out of the forest until *they* took it away."

"They?"

"The military, sir, long ago, another Myanmar, we hope."

As Ludwig looked around the bare room, it wasn't clear to him how long he would be able to stay in what felt like a cage. But he would have to make it through the weekend before he asked the director of Parami Prep to find another place for him. He didn't want to ask for an upgrade and act like another "ugly American" the moment he arrived.

"I told you it wouldn't be Far Rockaway."

He wasn't even sure he could make it through the weekend alone, so he asked Ko Ko to come back in the late afternoon after he had rested to take him on a tour of Yangon. If he still felt that the room was like a prison cell when they got back, he would check into a nearby three-star hotel he had seen on the internet before leaving America—Excel Pagoda.

* * *

Ko Ko arrived at early twilight in the Parami Prep van, a used VW, and asked Ludwig what he would like to see.

"I've only studied the map a little, Ko Ko, but show me the old British buildings and the famous Strand Road. And then I'd like to see where most of the students come from. I've been told that they come from poor village families. I've heard about Dalla Township on the other side of the Yangon River."

"I know a missionary there. I can take you to his child-care hostel. But you might prefer to see Inya Lake where Aung San Suu Kyi lived during her years of house arrest. She could see the American Embassy on the other side. Some people say she would signal to them with a lantern to let them know if she needed help."

"Another time. I'd first like to get a general sense of the city, so I'll know what to see during the next two weeks—the big picture. Please drive slowly."

"Still looking for 'big'!"

Quiet.

"Soon the rains will come, sir, and then it will be hard to see anything, but now you still can see the old British Empire." Ko Ko came to a stop at every major building. Flatbed trucks with exhausted laborers piled on each other like deflated tires, workers indistinguishable from tires, slowed traffic; and processions of monks, novitiates, and elders jammed the streets along Sule Pagoda and Merchant Roads.

"Here you can see our Raj, Doctor Fried."

"Please, call me Ludwig, Ko Ko."

"To the left, see the Irrawaddy Flotilla Building, and there, Lloyds Bank, but grandest of all, the British Embassy. Look, St. Mary's Cathedral."

Ludwig was tempted to ask Ko Ko to show him the synagogue, Musmeah Yeshua, which had to hire nearby Moslem merchants to make a *minyan*, but it was located in a remote part of Yangon, even as the whole city seemed to be a maze in which he might get lost forever without a guide. No Moses, he still could find himself wandering in the wilderness of this Buddhist metropolis.

"Get yourself a GPS, Luddy, you're no Kafka, you're my Yankee Clipper."

"*But you told me to stay home, remember?*"

"But you didn't listen, so now, be a mensch."

Easy for you to say, Pop, you never left the Garment Center. Spent your whole life on 37th Street. You never risked getting lost. You never woke up alone in Bangkok, Boston, Kerala, Kuala Lumpur, Manila. . . .

"What is this, geography lesson?"

I took them for you, so cut me some slack.

"I did better with slacks."

It's time to get serious.

Like his father, Ludwig was ambivalent about almost everything: stay home, join the navy and see the world; book a room at the Shangri-La, touch the hands of beggars who reached through the barred windows of night trains en route from Calcutta to Hyderabad; dream of dancing like Fred Astaire in the Rainbow Room, get up at dawn to harvest date-palms on a kibbutz in the Negev; write the great American novel, become a letter-writer in a remote Turkish village; love one good woman, play the field like Errol Flynn. . . .

The clock was ticking. The time had come to cross the Rubicon of his mixed and mixed-up feelings. He had the feeling that he could gain greater clarity about his life if he let Ko Ko show him how people lived on the other side of the Yangon River.

It wouldn't be the road to Mandalay, but that road, like other Manhattan fantasies—skyscrapers of the imagination that had arisen out of the memory of poverty and insignificance, memes that passed from father to son—hadn't led anywhere that made him feel whole and complete.

"Put the blame on meme?"

* * *

A thousand people waited at the Pansodan Jetty to board the ferry to Dalla. Its moss-covered and splintered hull didn't look to Ludwig as if it would be able to cut through the water, much less stay afloat.

A number of ill-fated sea journeys and drownings came quickly to mind—*The Caine Mutiny, Kon-Tiki, Lord Jim, Moby-Dick,* "The Convergence of the Twain"—so he paused with one foot on the creaky plank that might be, he thought, the last one he would step on.

"Is it safe, Ko Ko?"

"So far, sir."

"Your grandfather came to American steerage class in 1906, Luddy, huddled in a blanket near the engine room, you can do it."

Easy for you to say, you wouldn't even take the Brooklyn Ferry.

"Go ahead, be a Walt Whitman, see if I care."

I can't believe it, you've become an English major wherever you are.

"It's all in your mind, my *kaddish*, don't believe everything you think."

Ludwig waited for a few children to go ahead of him to lighten the weight on the plank and then, putting a hand on Ko Ko's shoulder for balance, stepped onto what felt like a tightrope joining the Canadian and American sides of Niagara Falls.

A boy in ragged clothing led them to a special section with folding chairs under a wide umbrella in the fore part of the ferry's upper deck, gave them a ticket, and held out his hand for a tip.

"Let him have one hundred kyats, sir."

"So much?"

"Only ten cents, his dinner."

Embarrassed, Ludwig gave the boy five hundred. The ferry began to move, rocking slowly. Downstream towards Moulmein and the open sea, the river had a silver sheen in the still bright light of early twilight, but the water close up was shadowy, sludgy, and squidgy along the bank where dead fish lay rotting. He wasn't sailing to Byzantium or any other literary port of call.

"Not chunkin' on the Irrawaddy either, but I saw worse on Hester Street, and your uncle Hy survived Corregidor, you can take it. Don't be a *schmendrick.*"

As the ferry eased towards the dock on the Dalla Township side of the river, a bamboo jetty that looked more like a collection of chopsticks than a slip, Ludwig signaled to Ko Ko for them to move close to the gangplank so they could be the first to get off. He didn't want to get crushed like a betel-nut between heavy baskets of linen, kitchen utensils, and rice before he saw what life was like on this side of the river. He had gone too far out of his comfort zone for him to get crushed like a sampan he once had seen splinter against the prow of a Star Ferry in Hong Kong's Victoria harbor.

He was only going to spend two weeks in this part of the world, but he didn't want it to be the end of his world. But if it was going to be the end of Ludwig Fried, he wanted it to be a meaningful one: a farewell to aloneness, literary *shtick*, rumination, self-enclosure, sense of loss, wordplay, quest for a home, escape from home, and a sample case of other tics.

He had dreamed long ago and far away of a world larger than the comfortable, narrow, and privileged one in which he had grown up, and now he was at the edge of this new world.

"So what's wrong with comfortable? You prefer maybe the Czar should come back and ship you to Siberia?"

But that same world hadn't prepared him for a life of exploration, but he had pressed on . . .

"Your uncle Hy, the *fresser*, became a presser when he came back from the war. He was a pinko, waiting for the revolution, but even he had to make a buck, even he fought the unions who wanted to kill us."

Living out, he now understood, his father's contradictory dream of escape from poverty and anonymity.

His father had been lost in the city and was afraid of getting lost among people he didn't know and who didn't know him. His father had been afraid to end up alone and unknown, unknown and alone, if he had boarded that freighter. He had been afraid to leave home.

But where *was* home? Once you had left it to make a life? Thomas Wolfe had failed to find it. Ludwig remembered an English folk saying, "A stag, when he is hunted, and near spent, always returns home."

Well, he was the hunter, unarmed, looking for a somewhat new life, and, although he often tired himself out with inner travel, he wasn't spent.

"I spent more at Belmont, Luddy, looking for a winner, give me a break."

Stop nagging.

Ludwig had thought of his father as a tough guy. After all, he knew some bookies, racetrack touts, corrupt union officials, models who were on the "light hustle," a phrase he once heard his father use. But it occurred to him now that his father hadn't gone anywhere by himself except Miami Beach once a year where his older brother lived.

"I should have gone to Hollywood. I could have been a producer."

I don't blame you, Pop. You did what you had to do.

"I should have gone to Hawai'i."

It's okay, it's okay. I'm out here for you.

He thought of some lines that his father had scribbled on the inside cover of a book of Robert Frost, given to Ludwig when he graduated college: *once kids who wanted to steal my ice and wagon attacked me, and they beat me black and blue, but I wouldn't let go of my wagon, never let go of your wagon.*

He regretted that he hadn't said, "You have a touch of the poet, Pop."

"No, you're the writer. I shipped, you submitted. I worked with material, you used paper, I had bolts of gabardine, you have bolts from the blue, me swatches, you notes, me returns, you rejections, but we're not so different, two dreamers, but I lost my nerve, you became nervous."

You're hard on yourself.

"So. Look who's talking?"

A row of thin, bare-chested bicycle-rickshaw riders, faces hidden beneath wide-brimmed straw hats, some with ankles bent from pedaling heavy loads, looked imploringly at him and Ko Ko as they stepped off the dock. Some pointed to their bent limbs, others held out hands, desperate, palms up.

"I know this one," Ko Ko said. "He won't cheat us and leave us nowhere if we don't pay more, and he's got a two-seater with an umbrella."

* * *

"What do you want to see, sir?"

"How children live, Ko Ko. Especially ones who have no families. I've read that many children are abandoned, especially girls, if they have a disability or parents can't afford them."

"That's true, but not all are mistreated. People need to know about some of the good, but unknown, people who look after them." Ko Ko told the driver to take them to the orphanage.

"Is he strong enough to take both of us?"

"In some ways he's stronger than us. He gets no credit for what he does, puts food on the table, that's all. He does what he has to do."

That's what you did, Pop. Gave up your dreams, so we could live, became a nobody so we could be somebody.

"So I become a nobody. What? You want to be like me? See if I care."

I thought you said, 'Never let go of your wagon.'

"That, too?"

Both?

"Give it a try."

I can't win.

"Maybe that's the point."

I don't know if you're Confucius, Charlie Chan, or a fortune cookie.

"Such a big difference?"

Enough already, this isn't the Milton Berle show.

The bicycle-rickshaw driver turned off a narrow paved lane onto a dirt path that led through a crowded stand of tall banana plants whose broad leaves brushed against Ludwig's shoulders.

The dappled light grew darker until the bicycle-rickshaw broke through the thick grove into a clearing where a fading sun cast light on a neatly trimmed courtyard in front of a bamboo hut with a wide porch.

A large wooden cistern stood in the middle of the clearing. A group of ten or twelve naked boys and girls ran around, splashed each other, and laughed. A thin, barefooted, white-haired man with opalescent eyes, wrapped in a pristine white sarong, stood on the porch, and watched. He smiled slightly, but softly.

"Tell me something about him," Ludwig said pointing to the man and then waving. "He has amazing eyes, like gems."

"More valuable than the ones you'll see in the Bogyoke Market. Biyot Kesh came from Malaysia to take care of them. He's a Christian missionary. His father was brought from south India, Tamil Nadu, to work on the rubber plantations in old Malaya, but made money, somehow, so his son could be educated. He never forgot his father's early years, near starvation, and poverty."

"What denomination?"

"His own, I think."

"You know a lot about him."

"Yes, I bring special guests here."

"Welcome," Biyot said. "I'll introduce you to the children as soon as I dry them off and they've put on their *loongis*."

"You watch them carefully."

"And watch over them, too. They have no one else yet, but I work with adoption agencies. Some of them will have real homes soon, I pray."

"Get your towels, children," Biyot called.

The children climbed out of the cistern and ran shouting towards a clothesline, grabbed fresh towels, and lined up before Biyot who carefully wrapped and dried off each one.

"Time to rest before dinner," he said. "Take your places on the porch."

"I should be as ordered by you," Ludwig said.

"They need to know that they belong somewhere."

"I know the feeling."

"Join them, sir, if only for a few minutes. I do sometimes. It's like meditation. Ko Ko knows what I mean."

Ludwig looked at Ko Ko who nodded. "You've come this far, sir, why not? You have nothing to lose."

Biyot unrolled bamboo mats for all the children and one for Ludwig.

"Please, sir, have a reflective and mindful rest," Biyot said, gracefully indicting a place for Ludwig. "You've come a long way. In the meantime, I want to show Ko Ko some of the new fruit trees that we've planted. We'll be back soon."

It seemed a little silly to Ludwig, but he didn't want to be rude, and after all he had come halfway around the world to learn something new, if possible, about himself and the world.

"That's my boy, a real learner, a Yale man."

Columbia, Pop, FDR, Lou Gehrig, Eisenhower, Obama, Paul Simon . . .

"OK, so be a big shot, see if I care."

Used to the routine, the children quickly lay silent and still. Ludwig hesitated, made sure no one was looking, and stretched out on the mat.

A light breeze brushed palm branches against the roof of the hut, and a wind-chime tinkled faintly in the distance. Otherwise, there were no sounds other than the children breathing and his own inner murmurings, but they soon subsided and a rare sense of calm came over him as if it were a waterless wave.

There had been a few moments like this in his life, but not for a long time, not since the Age of Aquarius, the "flower children." Once, then a young instructor, he had joined a group of students for a "love-weekend" in the Zoar Valley, south of Buffalo, to oppose by example the horrors of the Viet Nam war by listening to Judy Collins records and dancing, some naked, in the woods. At some point, it had begun to rain and students paired off and disappeared, as if they had known each other for years. Ludwig found himself standing alone next to a naked young woman with long hair. They looked at each other, hesitated, then held hands and went to her cabin where, chastely, they slept peacefully together in a sleeping bag.

When they broke camp and left the valley, he never saw her again, afraid that he might try to be less chaste the next time. Looking back, it had been an absurd experience, one of the era's many delusions, to think that this kind of retreat from history and communion in the woods could do anything to stop the napalming of villages.

But this almost druidic ceremony in the wood had enabled a generation to get through the war with the knowledge that there was an America they could believe in if only one could reach out and lovingly touch others.

The gathering in the woods had been an ineffectual, almost embarrassing, form of resistance to military madness, but the sense of community had left Ludwig with an unfulfilled need to escape the confines of his all too self-conscious world. He had been searching for a solution for decades and had done many foolish things over the years to find it. He had looked for communion in many of the wrong places. But now he felt that he had found it, if only for a moment, or a day, and he would do everything in his power not to lose it.

"So what's the 'it' big-shot?"

Tell their story, not mine.

As his breath rose and fell with the children on the porch who depended on Biyot for life support, he knew that his mission had changed. He had come to Myanmar to teach for two weeks, but now he knew that *he* would be the student.

Ludwig needed to learn what it felt like and meant to live as a helpless person, a nameless person among those whose lives would go unrecorded unless someone wrote about them and told their story.

"So where will you be in all of this? I thought you wanted your name in lights. You'll be a nobody."

Nothing and everything, Pop, I see that now. No one and everyone.

"Could be a bestseller, a real Pearl S. Buck, maybe a Steinbeck, you may have found a way."

Ludwig thought of a phrase from a book he had read in adolescence, "the we of me," but maybe the "we of me" made more sense now.

"This could be your fortune cookie, Luddy."

* * *

Looking at the skyline of Yangon as the ferry approached the Pansodan Jetty—the newly resurfaced facades of the Australian and British embassies rising above ramshackle warehouses and tin-shanties—he thought of Fitzgerald's words that had haunted him: "the city burst thunderously upon us in the early dusk—the whole white glacier of lower New York swooping down like a strand of a bridge to rise into Uptown. . . ."

That New York was gone . . .

"You can bet your bottom dollar."

. . . and Scott's words don't make sense in Yangon . . .

"Now you're talking."

And I can learn more here.

"What? And get lost again?"

No, find myself . . .

"Next thing I know, it will be *Yasnaya Polyana*. Lost, found, me, we, visible, invisible, famous, anonymous, I'm getting dizzy."

Don't worry, Ko Ko can be my guide, and you'll be with me. You're on my back, but you have my back, I see that now. Maybe I'll go to the peak of Hkakabo Razi at top of Kachin Sate where you can see India and China. Who knows? Maybe I'll see you.

"Forget miracles, you're on your own."

Ludwig had been in Yangon less than a day, but something had changed. It would still be a long weekend, and he would be lonely before he began teaching on Monday, but Ko Ko had said that Ludwig could call him for another local excursion.

If he got too lonely, he might reach out to the woman who had been sitting by the fountain. But if he did and she still reached out to him, he hoped he only would lie with her calmly, a home away from home. He wanted closeness now more than the sex-opiate.

He was beginning to understand that home could be anywhere. Lying next to the children on the porch and feeling that he was at one with them and could tell their story at some point made up just now for the windowless room at the *Lotus Boutique*, a room that now represented an enclosed space, one of many, that he wanted to leave.

He could check out, if he was too uncomfortable, but the children would remain helpless unless their story was told by him and others so that their world would change. These changes came slowly, and maybe not at all, but they only became possible when someone spoke up for them.

The time had come to disembark. With Ko Ko at his side, Ludwig no longer felt that he had to avoid the press of the crowd for fear of being crushed. In fact, he now wanted to become one of the crowd, and he needed to absorb the sounds and smells that would be useful to remember if he ever tried to write about his experience in Myanmar.

He had been in Yangon less than a day, but felt as if he had come close to the end of the world he had known.

It was hard to believe that he had come to the end of being the old Ludwig Fried after just one day in Yangon, but every now and then someone caught a break.

It was even imaginable that Ludwig Fried—ruminator, connoisseur of loss, archeologist of the self, reluctant traveler, epistolarian, antiquarian, scribbler, wondering and wandering Jew—might have a second act.

Time would tell. He still had to get through two weeks in Yangon. He only would know if he had become a somewhat different person when he returned to America and sat down to write something different that might make a difference.

Afterword
The Timely Birth of a Somewhat Comic Character

The inspiration for this introduction to *Second Time Around and other stories* (five related stories set in Israel) comes from Thomas Wolfe's overheated account in *The Story of a Novel* (1936) of his immersion in the creative process that culminated in *Of Time and the River*, one of his books that inspired me in adolescence to think, without any literary background or evidence of talent, of becoming a writer.

For Wordsworth, "The child is father of the Man."

For writers, the impulse to write precedes any notion of what they might write about or any clear sense that they possess the means to express themselves in a persuasive way, to say nothing of finding an audience and making a living.

One begins to write in the same way that a teenager might say to a friend, "I want to be a writer." It's a leap of faith, psychological bungee jumping, that may have some origin in our genetic and neurological makeup, an early trauma or primitive pleasure, an inexplicable identity theme that we don't yet, and may never, understand.

We make the decision to become writers with the same mixture of uncertainty and conviction that we bring to the title and first line of a new story, not sure where the words, each a prompt and echo, will take us.

Writers have the necessary belief that the beginning of a narrative foretells an end as well as the unwarranted conviction that the surprising end of a story already may be lodged in us waiting for a telling in which, looking back, there were no surprises. The origins of a creative idea remain a mystery.

But even when a work is finished and seems to possess aesthetic, dramatic, and intellectual wholeness, writers know that their work is incomplete. Every opening implies a previous conclusion, and every conclusion suggests a continuation. Writers may come to an end of a beginning, to echo Winston Churchill after the Battle of Britain, but there's never an end.

Every now and then a genius comes along—Proust, Thomas Wolfe, Gertrude Stein, Faulkner, Joyce—who believes that everything can be put into one book, but we can see how impossible that project is. *Finnegans Wake,* for all its brilliance, demonstrates the limits of this elusive project.

For some of these reasons, I want to tell the story behind my "Ludwig Fried" stories: what preceded them, what caused me to change directions as a storyteller, and where that leaves me now with respect to future writing.

After a month's stay in the late spring of 1975, I left The MacDowell Colony in Peterborough, NH, America's oldest artist colony (c. 1908), where both E.A. Robinson and Thornton Wilder spent many summers, with a manuscript in hand that would become in 1978 through a number of tortuous stages *Forgive the Father: A Memoir of Changing Generations* (New Republic Book Co.).

I returned to the colony in the autumn of 2016, forty-one years later, like Rip Van Winkle awaking as a writer, to revise a collection of fourteen short stories, *Exiles by Starlight,* that represents a significantly different kind of literary effort with respect to form and function.

I returned to do this in the same studio, Veltin, where E.A. Robinson had spent summers from1915 to 1934. A plaque commemorates his residency, "I shall have more to say when I am dead." I hoped to accomplish something similar in my lifetime without Robinson's grave prophecy.

If I believed in destiny, I would say that it had brought me to The MacDowell Colony and this stone studio because Edward MacDowell's "To a Wild Rose" had been one of the required pieces to recognize in Miss Taylor's P.S. 187 Manhattan's music education program; and the poem in Horace Mann School that most inspired me to write was Robinson's "Richard Cory."

In addition, an early published article that helped me earn tenure and a life as a writer within a university, a mixed blessing, as my stories reveal, was about Robinson's shorter poems ("Luke Havergal," "Mr. Flood's Party").

What happened to me as a writer between 1975 and 2016? Who was I as a writer in 1975 and who am I now as an author? The road from "writer" to "author" can be a solo version of Mao's long march. I hope the story of my stories, presented as an example and specimen, can shed glimmers of light on what it means to be a writer in America, the role of history, personal and shared, in a writer's development, and some of the complexities of the creative process.

A great deal goes into writing before and after publication, and the more we know about this history, the greater will be our appreciation of serious creative writing at a time when so many post-humanistic tendencies challenge its traditional civilizing role. We may, in fact, be in the twilight of a literary culture.

If nothing else, knowing more about the specifics of a veteran writer's life (and the artist in general) may help some young writers deal with the slings and arrows of inevitable early rejection on their ascent to the lookout of acceptance.

I drove back to Buffalo late spring 1975, where I had and still have an affiliation with the University at Buffalo, with the manuscript of the memoir I had worked on at the colony in a metal box to protect it in the event that I had a crack-up, not F. Scott Fitzgerald's, but a real collision since I tend to drift when I drive.

I had begun working on this memoir, then called *Gathering Evidence: After the 1960s*, in the early spring of 1974 in Berkeley where I was on sabbatical leave. I thought of it as a personal essay in its earliest stage. But then I received a letter from an editor in New York who had read an essay of mine in *The American Scholar*, "Quietude, Apocalypse, and Nostalgia" (America in the period 1950-1980) in which she asked me if I was writing a book.

It didn't take much reflection to decide on the spot to begin one—*Gathering Evidence*. The letter and prospect of publication with a major house in Manhattan lit a fire under me, and I wrote about four hundred pages in the next four months with an on-off sense of confidence in what I was working on since it was my first full-length book, not counting a doctoral dissertation.

I returned from Berkeley to Buffalo in the summer of 1975 and sent off the manuscript to my editor at George Braziller & Co., a small, but distinguished, publishing firm. My editor, the person who had written me the letter of query about a possible book, wrote a month later to say that the book wasn't acceptable in its present form. She then returned the manuscript with a list of suggestions for revision.

Academic year 1974-75 was an uplifting and dispiriting one for me. I wasn't convinced that I could bring the book to a publishable state, but I had fallen in love for the first time in many years with an ambitious younger woman who made it clear that she didn't want to be connected with a "loser." Either she was going to be a star or would hitch her wagon to one, or both.

So I made up my mind to marshal my resources and rework the book. I knew a writer, whom I had met during a difficult time in Mexico in the summer of 1968, who had been at The MacDowell Colony. Based on his report, it seemed like the perfect place to go with a completed manuscript that needed "only" revision. That word "only" can be deceptive.

I applied, was accepted, and drove to Peterborough, New Hampshire, at the end of the term, unhappy to separate myself from, let me call her, "Stella," but I knew that my only chance of staying in her life, of having a life with her, was to become a "success" in her eyes, if not Norman Podhoretz's. I didn't embrace all her values, but I wanted to embrace her, a common error of a January-May relationship.

After a month of hard editing (line-by-line changes and a reorganization of the whole text in which each chapter would be about one character, a fictional version of a real person who represented some aspect of the contemporary life), I drove back to Buffalo with the manuscript, as I've said, safely stowed in a metal box.

No cargo could have been more precious at that time: *Manuscript on Board.*

That box soon turned into a curio cabinet. A month later, my editor rejected the book in professionally cordial terms. "We regret to say that the memoir, though nicely crafted, lacks a certain dramatic intensity. It's not a page-turner. It's too ruminative. The narrator tries to enlarge experiences that remain, alas, less than monumental. This is not to say that a smaller press with a greater appreciation of style may not wish to add it to their list."

I was bitterly disappointed, of course, and apprehensive that Stella might see me as a terminal failure, twice rejected, a two-time loser. But I was grateful at least that I had a manuscript to work on, if only I could muster the self-confidence, renewed, and energy to work on it. I went back to the drawing board during 1975-76, a year that would be Stella's last with me before she decamped for graduate study to an Ivy League's Department of Comparative Literature.

With the help of a poet-friend, Pulitzer Prize winner Carl Dennis, who became my Maxwell Perkins, I was able to change the position of chapters so that the narrative unfolded in a more coherent fashion; and with his unfailing penchant for economy of expression, I was able in his words "to haul in the metaphoric spinnakers." Sons of big cities, neither of us could handle a tiller, but I understood what he meant.

It was a "pretty good year," as Frank Sinatra says, but by the time I was ready to send the manuscript around again in the fall of 1976, Stella had fallen for one of her instructors, a well-known literary "theorist," although *of what* still puzzles me.

She had, in one stroke and *coup de grâce*, become a disciple of Jacques Derrida and deconstructed me. If there was any irony in this, I didn't see it at the time. It was a *coup de grâce* without any grace for me. She may have believed in my possible future, but not my present. Her farewell note said, "If you become famous, I may regret what I'm doing."

With little hope, but propelled by the need both to prove to myself that I wasn't a loser and as a tincture of revenge, I began to circulate the manuscript in the winter of 1977. I knew that I would be giving up on myself if I failed to believe in my creative work, and I knew that only creative work could compensate, to some degree, for a life loss.

Still, every time I put stamps on the manuscript, I felt as if I were licking my wounds, knowing that this form of treatment wasn't helping me heal. Only something like "success," that ticket to self-esteem in America, would put salve on the wound of rejection.

Grief, self-pity, preoccupation with teaching, psychotherapy, several ice storms, working out, brief encounters with any woman who might help me forget Stella—these elements and some others, suppression and repression, would put the circulating manuscript out of mind for weeks at a time. But when the fate of the book reentered consciousness, I felt as if I was about to fall off a promontory in the Adirondacks, maybe Whiteface, and wondered if I was wise to keep looking for a publisher.

Then one late afternoon in February, the coldest time of the year in Buffalo, I got a call from an editor at the then New Republic Book Company who said that she liked my book up to a certain point. "You capture some of the spirit of the 1960s, I know, I was part of it, the Zoar Valley, but the narrative lacks intensity. You mention Mt. Rushmore, but the story isn't big enough. It requires revision. Are you willing to make changes?"

I felt as if I were being inserted into Kafka's "Penal Colony" or put on an inquisitorial rack so that saying "Yes" would be a self-punishing act; but I knew, of course, that to say "No" would have been more masochistic.

Back to work again. I submitted the revised manuscript and was told a month later that it still needed a little more work. "Please come to D.C., we can sit side-by-side and make those changes." The prospect of physical proximity seemed to be a good sign (how could she reject me if we exchanged body warmth?), so I flew to Washington and stayed at the Tabard Inn with less confidence in the future than some of Chaucer's pilgrims.

When I arrived at her office and sat down, she eased the manuscript towards me. It had about one hundred paper clips inserted where she wanted changes. Each one looked like a needle and syringe for drawing blood.

Each time a correction was made and a clip removed, I felt as if a little less pain lay in wait for me. Two days passed, and when the last clip was removed, I wondered if I had any blood left.

Well, the book was published, created a small ripple in Buffalo—radio and TV interviews, some press commentary—but not a splash in New York or any other large literary pond.

At the same time, I felt that I now was a real writer, if a minor one, in the world's eyes. As my daughter once said, "C'mon, Dad, how many people have even published one book?" It also helped me get promoted to "full" professor. But I knew that it would be imperative for me, in the shadow of my experience, to look for a "big" topic if I wanted to be taken seriously as a writer—clearly, my life-quest, the Holy Grail for this son of the Bronx.

The two editors, in different ways, had made that clear. I needed to find a larger context both for my creative nonfiction and my fiction. I hadn't found a sufficiently dramatic way in *Forgive the Father: A Memoir of Changing Generations* to enlarge my family's history.

Arthur Miller faced something like this challenge in *Death of a Salesman*, but he found a way, like Chaplin, to enlarge the status of the "little man." Gifted writers always find a way through what Henry James calls the "alchemy of art" to solve problems. I possessed lesser talent and needed some help.

Waiting for a big topic, I abandoned writing for quite a few years, but then in 2004, I served as the advisor to Jaroslav, a Fulbright visitor from Presov, Slovakia. I learned prior to his coming to Buffalo, as the result of his research, that a great-uncle of mine (of whom my mother had no knowledge), Ludwig Fried of Zbecno, Czech Republic, had been transported during the Holocaust to Terezinske on Feb. 22, 1942 and killed at Majdanku on Sept. 3, 1942.

When Jaroslav came to Buffalo, he gave me a thick packet of documentation. I promised myself then that I would go to Zbecno at some point to learn more about the life and fate of Ludwig Fried and two brothers and a sister who had not emigrated to America with my mother's father and three of his sisters.

This revelation about my family's lost history changed my relation to modern history, writing, and sense of identity. If I needed a "big topic," I had found one that needed to be treated with respect and ingenuity.

Without working this out fully, I found myself inventing a Jewish American character, "Ludwig Fried," whose life is shadowed and rendered comically ironic, with respect to uncertainty and suffering, in contrast to his doomed European counterpart.

To date, I have written eighteen stories, including a novella, about "Ludwig" over a period of fourteen years. All the stories in this collection, dramatize through rumination, personal and historical, the experience of this wondering and wandering character, "Ludwig Fried," whose life is lived against the background of post-Nuremberg Trial history and all the horrific revelations about the *Shoah* that have come to light since that time through documentary film, archival research, memoirs, and, of course, the testimony of survivors.

Ludwig's suffering pales in comparison with the nameless inhumanity of the Holocaust, so that any writer would hesitate to make the comparison. At the same time, all characters are entitled to the reality of their own experience.

Ludwig's anxieties and sense of displacement, I realized, real in themselves, had to be seen as microscopic in the lens of history; yet, in another sense, his "small" suffering gains its significance from the larger history.

I left the MacDowell Colony for Buffalo after a brief "emergency residency," an artist's ER retreat, in September 2016 with a revised manuscript of my stories. As I drove away from the colony, past the pastoral setting of Edward and Marion MacDowell's gravesite, a large boulder that one approaches through a series of ivy-entwined arbors, I thought of Tennyson's "Ulysses": "Yet all experience is an arch where through gleams that untraveled world."

I had as much hope invested in the possible publication of *Exiles by Starlight* as I did in 1975 when I returned with *Forgive the Father*. But the issue of acceptance or rejection felt less dramatic now. I was near the beginning of a career as a writer in 1975, and it seemed as if that career could be cancelled if my memoir was fated to end up in a drawer. In truth, I wasn't sure that I would continue to write if I failed to get my first non-academic book into print.

I looked at that time into the future and saw a fork in the road: Success-Failure. Now I look back at myself looking into the future and know that success and failure are relative terms, as much as one still might seek fame; but only writers know if they have fulfilled their expectations about a work, if they have managed to put "into" the world in articulate terms what is "in" them. They know that only Dr. Johnson's "test of time" will confirm whether what one has written will find a place in history.